Just then … e in her life ha…

The change ha… when she'd run into Adam her first … Wolf Lake. And another change was coming tomorrow.

"Everyone I know seems to be going through some sort of upheaval in their lives, some minor, some very major," he said. She heard him exhale and instead of looking over at him, she turned to the side window and the night outside. "Jack and Mallory have endured huge changes and their lives will never be the same."

She was uneasy with the conversation. She didn't want to think about the way lives could be altered forever in a second. She was living through that horror. Her fingers were aching where they clutched her purse, and she forced her hand to relax on the worn leather. "Sometimes we don't have choices in things like that," she said softly.

"True, but I wish Jack would talk about what's happening with him. He's so closed, and handling it on his own. That's no good for anyone."

"It's how he deals with things," she said, knowing she had no choices about her actions. She'd had to leave, to keep moving and stay low. She never dreamed she'd end up in a truck in a small town with a cop and not be under arrest. That last thought made her want to either laugh or scream. She wasn't sure which one was the right reaction. So instead, she said, "Everyone has to do what they have to do."

Dear Reader,

A very dear friend of mine said something many years ago that I didn't quite understand until I started to write and deal with characters on a personal level. *"Adam and Eve had different kids."* I thought it was a flip way of saying everyone is as different as everyone else, which is probably true. But I didn't fully appreciate the basic truth of that statement until I started writing about the Carsons of Wolf Lake.

Three brothers, Jackson, Gage and Adam, are heading in three different directions, all attached to their heritage, but each with his own unique needs and dreams for his future. Brothers who were raised by the same parents in the same place, Wolf Lake, yet brothers who embraced particular visions of what constituted "perfect."

That is until they met the women who would change their lives for the better. It turns out the differences in each brother proves to be the foundation for a relationship that will survive just about anything. A happily-ever-after might be everyone's goal from childhood, but the journey is what makes a person and shows him or her what this life is all about, including a love that lasts forever.

I hope you enjoy the Carson family's journey.

Mary Anne Wilson

Mary Anne Wilson

A Question of Honour

MILLS & BOON

Published in Great Britain 2014
by Mills & Boon, an imprint of Harlequin (UK) Limited,
Eton House, 18-24 Paradise Road, Richmond, Surrey, TW9 1SR

ISBN: 978 0 263 24485 4

33-0214

Harlequin (UK) Limited's policy is to use papers that are natural, renewable and recyclable products and made from wood grown in sustainable forests. The logging and manufacturing processes conform to the legal environmental regulations of the country of origin.

Printed and bound in Spain
by Blackprint CPI, Barcelona

MARY ANNE WILSON

is a Canadian transplanted to Southern California, where she lives with her husband, three children and an assortment of animals. She knew she wanted to write romances when she found herself rewriting the great stories in literature, such as *A Tale of Two Cities,* to give them happy endings. Over her long career she's published more than thirty romances, had her books on bestseller lists, been nominated for Reviewer's Choice Awards and received a career nomination in romantic suspense.

For Kaetlyn, who shows me constantly that life is worth whatever it takes to make it work.

I love you more than you can ever say you love me!

CHAPTER ONE

Chicago, Illinois

FAITH SIZEMORE STRODE quickly along the upscale residential street located a block from Lake Michigan. A light snow had just begun to fall. As she headed for the only home she'd ever known, she carried the knowledge that she was about to make a decision that would affect the rest of her life.

She moved unnoticed along the snowy sidewalk. She'd deliberately changed her appearance and was relieved that it seemed to have worked. Gone were the sleek designer clothes, her usual calf-high leather boots and the expensive shoulder bags she habitually carried.

She'd never been fond of her diminutive size—five feet two inches and barely one hundred pounds—but now she thought it might work in her favor and that it gave new meaning to the expression "staying under the radar."

Gone were the makeup, the leather gloves and diamond studs she always wore, a gift from her father when she graduated from college. Plain and simple had been her goal. She was plain and simple right then as she neared the front of her family's historic town house. The reporters that had dogged her every step for the past four months were clustered outside the high wrought-iron gates, and she knew this would be the real test

The "new" Faith was hunched into the wind, her chin tucked into the fleece collar of her definitely unstylish wool parka. Slim jeans were little protection against the biting cold and wind-driven snow, but her chunky boots took the slippery street with ease. A dark watch cap was pulled low on her head, almost covering her ebony hair, transformed from long, sleek locks to a cap of crazy curls that didn't even touch the collar of her jacket.

She didn't slow as she got to the group of reporters and the nearby protesters. She didn't look at the house or the six-foot tall gates. Instead, she kept going, muttering,

"Excuse me," over and over again as she made her way through the crowd.

Suddenly, she felt something hit her shoulder and she turned, coming face-to-face with one of the protesters, a woman who held a sign that read *Greed* Is a Four-Letter Word. Faith thought it best not to say anything and picked up her pace. She was almost at the corner. Behind her the woman screamed, "Death to corporate greed!"

The security guard hired by her father was keeping an eye on the crowd. He spotted her but gave no indication that he recognized her, yet he'd seen her every day for the past month. She let out a long sigh.

She hadn't realized how tense she'd been about doing this until that moment, and now, surprisingly, she felt vaguely faint. The feeling fled when she turned the corner onto the side street that ran along the extensive property where the hundred-year-old house stood.

She walked purposefully, nearing a narrow gate that fit snugly into the fence and led to an arch cut in the brick wall of the garage, a converted carriage house. She kept going but chanced a look back, noticing her boot impressions in the snow. No one was there. In one fluid motion, she reversed directions and retraced her steps to the gate. She quickly put in a security code on a pad, and the gate clicked, then slowly swung open.

She went through and carefully closed the gate so that it wouldn't make any noise. She heard the lock reset with a soft humming sound, and then she turned to hurry across the snow-shrouded terrace. Ignoring a set of French doors that led to the formal dining room, she approached a single oak door almost out of sight at the top of two cement steps.

Another keypad surrendered to her code, and she stepped inside, into the almost total darkness of the utility room where deliveries were made. She didn't need to turn on any lights because she knew the space by heart. Quietly, she moved through the kitchen to the back stairs that led to the upper floors. There was her bedroom, but she sidestepped it and went directly to her favorite room, the library.

She loved the dark wood paneling, the bookshelves soaring to the ceiling. A huge bay window overlooked the front gardens and the gates that blocked the main entrance to the property. Just being on the inside made her feel safer. When she was a child, she would curl up in one of the rich leather chairs by her father's massive antique desk and read while he worked.

This was the only home she'd ever known, and her chest tightened as the thought flashed in her mind that this might be her last time here. She wished she could just sit in the chair and read or watch her father at his computer, instead of making such a huge decision about her future. She swallowed to try to ease the tightness, then glanced inside the partially opened library door.

She saw her father sitting behind his desk, as always. He was hunched forward, white shirtsleeves rolled up, and the eerie bluish cast from one of his computer monitors bathed his features in its pale glow. The only other light came from a low desk light. Even so, she could see the way her father was working his jaw, and the intent frown that drew his dark eyebrows together. He seemed totally involved in what he was reading on the screen, and she thought he didn't know she was there. Then he released a low hiss of air and slowly swiveled his chair toward her.

He was absolutely still for a moment, and then he stood awkwardly as if his legs were stiff. Without a word, he crossed the room to meet her near the open door. She took a shaky breath as he came closer, inhaling the mingled scents of the fire blazing in the fireplace and the hint of pine in the air.

A two-foot-tall live Christmas tree stood by one of the windows against burgundy velvet drapes that had never been closed until recently. The tree looked pathetic. It made her wish she hadn't insisted on getting it. She foolishly had thought that it would help them to not totally ignore Christmas this year. But since it was the only Christmas decoration in the house, its puny presence only magnified how far they'd fallen from a normal life.

"Faith," her father said in a quiet voice as he caught her in a hug that was so tight she could barely take a breath. But she savored it, storing it up in her memory to grab when she would need it. He finally released her, smiling at her, but the expression didn't reach his intent blue eyes. "I didn't think you were going to come back here for a while."

At five feet ten inches, he wasn't an unusually tall man and his frame had always been trim from playing squash or from running. But to Faith he had always seemed like a giant. After her mother had died when Faith was four, he'd been her security, a man who could fix her world with the wave of a hand; her rock, the one person she trusted completely; and most of all, her dad.

Now that was all changing before her eyes. He was diminishing, as if the pressures of his life over the past four months were crushing him downward slowly and painfully. His once lightly graying hair was just as thick, but the color was now pure white. The lines etching his eyes and mouth had deepened considerably, and any tan he'd had, had faded away, leaving his skin almost ashen.

Faith had never doubted that her father could conquer the world, yet here he was fighting for his life. She felt that sense of loss completely and refused to make things worse for him.

She skimmed off her woolen cap. "Those vultures out front are not as good as they think they are," she said, trying to lighten the mood. "And neither is that guard. I went right past all of them, even one of the protesters, and none of them even blinked."

Any trace of a smile on her dad's face was gone as he uttered, "You cut your hair." He turned away from her and went to his desk. He dropped heavily into his leather chair and swiveled back and forth until his gaze met hers. She could see pain and sadness in his expression and it was almost her undoing. "Did you get subpoenaed?" he asked flatly.

"No, I haven't." She claimed a leather chair across from him. "I haven't heard anything, but Baron is on his way over here," she said quickly. "I would have called to let you know, but..." She shrugged nervously as she tugged off her gloves and pushed them into her jacket pockets. Baron Little, the head of her father's legal team, had insisted on meeting with her, and she thought she knew why. What he had to say probably wasn't good. "I was afraid someone might be listening."

"Everything here was swept this morning. It's clean, at least for now." His eyes narrowed on her hair. "You haven't had short hair since you were a year old, and suddenly..."

She had thought she'd never do more than trim her hair, but that had changed. "I wanted to fool all of them, and I did." She motioned to the tall windows covered by the heavy drapes. "I wanted to be here with you when Baron told me what was happening." She tried to keep her voice steady. "You haven't heard from him about the subpoena, have you?"

He sat forward so abruptly that some papers skittered off the desk and settled on the thick Turkish rug. "No, but the grand jury is being impanelled. Got word yesterday about that. They're going to file charges. It's a given." He raked his thick hair with his fingers. "They have to."

Faith couldn't even swallow, her throat was so tight. "Maybe they won't," she offered up, but knew she was being delusional.

"They will," he said with resignation, "but I won't let them pull you any more deeply into this. Besides, you can't tell them anything they don't already know." He spoke evenly, and she knew that he believed that. "What would they gain, really?"

She wanted to point out that she had been and still was in the middle of things since that awful day four months ago. Federal agents had swarmed LSC Investments, where her father had worked for over twenty years and had been a full partner for all but four of those years. That day everything had changed.

She'd been in her glass-walled office talking to a prospective client about investments when she'd heard the loud voices and confusion in the main area. Then an assistant marshal had been at her door, telling her to step away from her desk. She'd been among the group of employees to be escorted off the premises, forced to leave everything behind. Her father and the other partners hadn't been so fortunate. She hadn't seen her father again for almost twenty-four hours. The Feds had confiscated everything to do with the business, from client files, computers, logs, employee workups and all banking information, both domestic and foreign.

Now, after four torturous months, there was going to be a decision about what charges would be filed against the partners, two of the company's financial officers and seven other employees. A bad dream had irrevocably turned into a nightmare. Her world and her father's were taken over by lawyers and bail and affidavits and depositions, and her father was central to it all.

Accusations of mishandling clients' money,

obstructing justice and fraudulent practices came down like a stinging hailstorm. And even with one of the best legal teams in the country working to prove her father's innocence, she had watched him sink deeper and deeper into the abyss.

She swallowed hard, hoping her face didn't give away her sickening fear. He still didn't know what she knew. She found she couldn't tell him. And now… A week ago, Baron Little had mentioned that her name was being bandied about to receive a subpoena to testify in front of the grand jury. That had come out of the blue for her, shattering any hope she had of being able to avoid that very thing.

She couldn't tell the attorney anything, not when she couldn't trust that he wouldn't have to reveal what she knew to the prosecution. She wasn't about to tell anyone about eight months ago when she'd gone to her father's office to find out when he could leave for home. A simple thing.

Even when she'd arrived outside his office and heard the raised voices of two of the partners, she hadn't thought much of it. They'd had disagreements over the years. She'd been ready to turn around and just go home on her own, but she stopped when she heard Winston Linz, a founder in the company, speak harshly to her father. "You're not simon-pure, Ray. None of us are. You're in this with us, and it's working. Leave it alone. The commission from this deal will be enough for all of us to retire on someday."

Her father's voice had come back with burning anger in it. "Don't you threaten me, Win. Don't you even try!"

"Works both ways. If all you've done comes out, you're dead in the water. So do what you have to do and make it happen, or—"

"Or?" her father demanded.

"Or it's over, at least for you."

She heard another voice talking about an account of a client she had never heard of before, Kenner Associates. It sounded as if the man was reading from a file about a new investment account. He finished with "They want it done. They want it finalized and they do not want anyone screwing it up."

"You don't have a choice, Ray," Linz said bluntly.

All of them were silent for a long moment, then her father spoke again in a tone that sounded calm, but Faith knew otherwise. "It will be finished. I will make sure of it personally with Mason. I'll sew it up."

She'd walked away, not understanding and not asking anyone about it, not even her father when he eventually got home that evening. Even though they worked in the same company, doing the same things, hers less important than his, they both took care of their own business. He never questioned her about any of her clients. She would never question him about his dealings. And it was forgotten until the world exploded and that same client, Kenner Associates, came up again.

It had turned out that Kenner Associates was a year-long sting operation, executed to trap those involved in substantial financial misdeeds. Faith had been sick, immediately knowing that if she told anyone about what she'd heard, it could be the end of her father. It showed knowledge and complicity with the others in the core deal where violations had occurred.

Her testimony, if she ever had to give it, could be the last nail in the coffin of Raymond Sizemore. She would be responsible for sending her father to prison. And she couldn't do that. She wouldn't. She was also a horrible liar, so not being truthful on the stand was out.

She tasted bitterness in her throat. "I need to know if I'll be subpoenaed to testify or not," she said earnestly. "I can't."

He watched her intently. "Just tell them the truth," he said in a low voice. "That's all they want."

She flinched at his words. The truth. Yes, she could tell the truth. She bit her lip hard. "You know it's not like that. They pick and choose. Reinvent how things appear."

"Faith, this is the Federal government, not some quack sheriff in a Podunk town that you'd be tangling with as if you'd gotten a traffic ticket. And if you don't testify, it will make you look as if you're guilty of something, which you aren't. Refusing a subpoena is as good as putting yourself in jail." He hit the top of his desk with the flat of his hand and the sudden sound made Faith jump. "You can't. I won't let you do that."

She wasn't about to refuse to obey a subpoena. It wouldn't get that far. "I won't be subpoenaed. I'll be gone. I told you that I'd just disappear." And she knew they'd find her, but the time between then and now was what she could control. Until whatever indictments were secured, she couldn't be anywhere close to anyone in the case, or in this city, or even the state.

"I'll deal with what I have to deal with," she stated simply. "I'm twenty-six, all grown up, an adult, and I can do this. I will do this if I have to." He'd done so much for her all of her life. He'd loved her and cared for her as a single parent, encouraged her to go to college when he realized she had his knack for figures and planning. With her newly minted MBA degree, he'd paved the way for her to join his firm, work her way up, and become an associate with her own office and list of clients she advised.

Sorrow overtook his expression now. "Why?" he asked.

"Because I won't hurt you, even indirectly," she said. "When Baron gets here, we'll know if I have to do anything beyond stand by you."

As if her mention of the attorney had conjured him, there was a soft chime from one of the computers. Her dad turned the monitor enough for her to see the image on it. Baron

Little, a huge man made to appear even bigger by the expensive overcoat he'd chosen to wear, stared up into the security camera by the main entry. He flicked a wave at them and her dad hit a key. They waited for him in the library. They heard the front door open and close. Heavy footsteps sounded in the hall, and then Baron Little, the brains behind her father's defense team, came into the room.

The man's size belied his surname and made the room seem smaller. He glanced from Raymond to Faith as he came to the desk. "I was hoping you were able to get here without a problem," he said to Faith, his gaze taking in her altered appearance, but he didn't say a thing about it.

"Well?" Faith managed to get out, hating asking, but anxious to know what direction her life would take after tonight.

The large man had been undoing the heavy buttons on his overcoat, but his hands stilled at the single word. "The grand jury is set, and they should be sending out a server in two days. You're going to be on the list."

Her heart sank. Faith had to will herself to get to her feet. "Thank you," she whispered, and then she looked at her dad. "I'm leaving." When he started to argue, she stopped him. "Please, no, I have to. I had it worked out in case I needed to, and now I do." She felt almost numb as she moved around the desk to bend down and give her father a kiss on the cheek. "I'll call when I can. I'd never do anything to hurt you," she said. "I love you."

He grabbed her hand. "Where are you going?"

"Away," she said matter-of-factly, not wanting him to know anything. This was all her doing.

He let go of her and reached into a drawer to his left. He took out a large red square envelope with a Christmas bell design on it and offered it to Faith. "I'd hoped I wouldn't have to give you this early, but…"

She took the card from him, hugging it tightly to her chest without opening it. "I didn't get you anything," she said as a tear rolled down her cheek.

Her dad stood, brushed at the moisture on her face with an unsteady hand, then pressed her to him. "As long as you're my daughter and believe in me, I've got all I need," he uttered. "Merry Christmas, Angel."

Faith forced herself to leave without looking back. She moved quickly. Her dad's use of the nickname he'd given her as a baby hurt her so much. She brushed past the attorney and would have left if Baron hadn't said her name.

"Faith."

She paused and closed her eyes, keeping her back to the room. "I can't tell you anything," she said.

"I don't want you to. Just be safe, and if you need anything..." He touched her shoulder and she saw him hold out a business card to her. "On the back, my personal numbers. Use one of them if you have to."

She accepted the business card without looking at it and slipped it into her jacket pocket. The attorney spoke again. "Hold on, I got the files you asked for." She had almost forgotten he'd promised to get her copies of files from the Kenny setup that would be used in any case against her father. She turned to see Baron with a thumb drive. "Lots on there," he said.

She took it from him and, without looking at her father, walked away. She retraced her path and checked the security screen by the side door. No one. Only falling snow and leafless trees bending in the growing wind.

Minutes later she reached the old import she'd bought from a private party two days ago. She couldn't register the car in her name, so she chose not to register it. The tags were good until June, so she felt she had enough time to use it and keep her name off the title. She'd parked seven blocks away from the house and felt slightly breathless from the walk by the time she slipped behind the wheel.

She got the engine going, then set the heater on high, which, she'd found on the way there, meant warm enough. Sinking back into the seat, she stared at the red foil envelope in her hands and watched the snowflakes melting on the surface.

She tugged the sealed flap open with hands that were less than steady and looked inside. There was a small plastic card and a flat box in green foil. She caught the plastic card between her fingers and pulled it out. She almost cried at her father's ability to hate what she was doing and yet help her if she had to do it, even when he was afraid for her. She'd emptied her back account and had enough cash to keep going for a good amount of time. But only her father would think of the one thing she hadn't considered.

She was holding an Illinois driver's license with her picture and vitals, the same ones on her real license. She was five feet two inches, 105 pounds, with black hair and blue eyes. But what wasn't right was the name, Faith Marie Arden, or the address, somewhere in Rockford, Illinois. Arden had been her mother's maiden name, and she didn't even know anyone in Rockford.

She wasn't about to try to figure out how her father had managed to get the license; she was just grateful that he had. "Thank you, Dad," she whispered as she put it in her wallet. She opened the glove compartment and slipped her valid license under the sales papers for the car. She sat back and reached inside the foil envelope again to take out the only thing left. The box.

It had a single strand of ribbon around it, and she undid it, letting it fall to her lap. Opening the box, her eyes filled with hot tears as she took out a delicate gold bracelet with a single charm on it. It was a locket in the shape of a heart. Her mother's. Something her father valued beyond measure. But he'd given it to her. Through a blur of tears, she manipulated the tiny lock and the heart fell open. Inside was a photo of her when she was just born, and on the other side was a photo of her mother and father on their wedding day.

When she had been very young, her father would open the locket and tell her stories about everything he could remember about Marie Arden. She heard how they met, fell in love and how thrilled they were when their daughter was born three days before Christmas.

She studied the images of three people at the start of their lives together. Her mother was gone. Her father was in real danger of being destroyed. And she was driving away from the only person who mattered in her life. She started to drop the bracelet back into the box, but spotted a folded piece of paper lying on the bottom.

She took it out, opened it and read, "Merry Christmas, Angel. You were the best Christmas present ever. Dad."

Faith swiped at her face again, wishing she could wear the bracelet, but afraid to. It was so delicate. Still, she had it with her. She put the note and bracelet away and pushed the box into the glove compartment.

As she pulled away from the curb, she felt the tires slip on the fresh snow, then gain purchase. She was heading south, away from Chicago. She paid no attention to the Christmas decorations adorning the streets, and by the time the city was in her rearview mirror, she felt an overwhelming sadness mixed with a strong conviction that she was doing the best thing for everyone.

"Merry Christmas, Mom and Dad."

CHAPTER TWO

Santa Fe, New Mexico

ADAM CAMERON HAD ARRIVED in town an hour ago and sat alone in a coffee shop near the airport. He was waiting for his ride home to Wolf Lake, two hours northeast. He'd chosen a booth by the window that overlooked the street, keeping an eye out for a police cruiser, the one his childhood friend John Longbow told him he would be driving.

John had been surprised by Adam's call a few days ago, assuming that his friend would be back according to his normal timetable—get home the day before Christmas and leave as soon as he could.

To be honest, Adam had been surprised by his own decision to arrive home early. But it had ended up being an oddly easy one for him to make.

When he'd called home to let his mother know when he'd be there, he'd figured she wouldn't be happy but that she'd understand how busy he was. And besides, she would have Jack, his older brother, and Gage, his younger brother, there, which would take some of the sting out of her disappointment. Lo and behold, he'd been wrong, very wrong.

The waitress appeared with his coffee. A cute blonde who never stopped smiling or calling him "hon" as she set the steaming mug in front of him. "You new around here, hon?" she asked with that smile still blazing.

Adam didn't flirt well. He'd always thought that if something happened, it happened, but working to make it happen didn't sit well with him. *Been there, done that,* he thought as he poured cream into his coffee. He hated playing games. That was why he liked relationships with no ties and no complications. He would admit to anyone that he had commitment phobia. He liked freedom and moving along when he had the urge to go. His latest stop had been Dallas, on the police force there, but already he was thinking about making a change, maybe heading to California.

The waitress was waiting for an answer, and he was vague. “I’m just here for a few days,” he said as he picked up his mug and turned back to the window.

He heard the waitress sigh, and in the window watched the reflection of her walking away. Then Adam’s image overlapped hers. With his ebony hair combed straight back from his sharp-featured face, one half of his heritage was emphasized, and it wasn’t the fair-skinned Irish side that rose to the surface. He could see his mother’s Navajo ancestry that defined him in more ways than one.

All three Carson boys were chiseled from the same mold physically, with decent height, tanned skin and bold features. But their characters were uniquely different. Jack was the homeboy who loved the land. Adam was the restless one, and their younger brother, Gage, was passionate about building anything. But right then it was Jack who filled Adam’s thoughts as he waited.

That simple call to his mother, but Jack answering the phone, and everything changed when he heard his brother’s voice come over the line.

As he picked up his mug, he spotted the

police cruiser emblazoned with *Wolf Lake P.D.* on the door and John behind the wheel. Adam put down his coffee, slapped a five-dollar bill on top of his tab and then headed for the door. The waitress calling after him, "You come on back, hon, you hear?" He let the doors shut on her voice and he approached John, who had gotten out of the cruiser.

The men hugged, thumped each other on the back and got inside the car. "Welcome back, man," John said, and in that moment, Adam experienced something unsettling and unusual for him. A huge wave of homesickness washed over him. He couldn't remember that ever happening to him before, even as a kid. He'd always looked beyond the horizon.

Until now.

Adam murmured, "I appreciate the ride."

"Glad to do it," John said as he swung the cruiser out into traffic.

"Did you really have business in the city?" he asked, eyeing the man's dark uniform, which looked rumpled from prolonged wear.

"Of course I had business in Santa Fe. Besides, I like having good company when I make this trek."

They had barely gone a few blocks before Adam's cell phone rang. He fished it out of his pocket and glanced at the ID, expecting it to be work or even his mother. But he did a double take. The call was from his kid brother, Gage, and that surge of homesickness came again.

"Hey," he heard over the line after he answered the call. "What are you up to?"

"Just off a plane in Santa Fe and heading for home."

Gage didn't sound surprised by that statement. "Good, Mom's looking forward to it."

"Mom called you about me coming back now?"

"No, actually. John did," Gage answered. Adam was confused.

He turned to look at John, who was staring dead ahead out the window. "You called Gage about me coming early?"

John glanced dark eyes at him and nodded. Without saying a thing, he went back to his driving.

"Why?"

No hesitation. "Jack."

Adam closed his eyes. There were no secrets in Wolf Lake. Everyone knew the Carson family's history and circumstances, especially their good friend John. "Go on," Adam said into the phone.

Gage spoke quickly. "I'm real busy here." Where that was, he didn't say. Gage's design and construction company worked all over the globe, and Gage, who was a hands-on owner, went wherever the jobs were being done. "I won't be home for Christmas, so I was glad to hear you would be."

There was a commotion almost blotting out Gage's voice. "Hold on," he said, then, "Listen, Adam, I have to go. Just call me when you get there and see Jack."

Adam barely had time to say "Okay" to his kid brother before the line went dead. He put his phone back into his pocket and looked at John again. "Why did you call him about Jack?"

John shrugged. "Worried."

Adam was worried, too. He was worried enough to not only come home early, but block out a month of sick leave with the police force to give himself time to figure out what he needed to do to help his older brother.

John kept talking. "He's not himself, although, I understand that after what he's gone through. But he rides off for days alone into the high country. He's at work on and off, mostly off, but he's still living in the apartment above his law office. Going to tell me why you're here early? What got to you to make you do that?"

Adam noted the landscape changing as they left Santa Fe. The old-world charm of the city, with its adobes and pueblolike housing clusters, morphed into vast, sprawling land, cut here and there by massive buttes and towering mesas. Home. He swallowed hard. "I talked to Jack. He was at Mom and Dad's place, and he answered the phone when I called."

"He asked you to come home?"

"No, he'd never do that. It wasn't even anything Jack said, not really." Adam remembered his brother talking about anything and everything except himself. His voice was different, flat and uninvolved in what he was saying. "When I asked him about some things, I could tell he's not doing well."

"He's grieving, Adam."

"I know. But it's been a year and a half since Robyn was killed in the accident, and he's not moving on. You said he's staying by himself mostly. He lets Maureen take care of his cases, and those rides alone…" He thought of Jack going to law school, leaving the town for an extended time, then coming home, falling in love with Robyn and making a life with her that looked perfect.

They had lived in the loft over the offices in the center of town, everyone expecting they'd start building on Wolf land when they had kids. But there had been no kids, and not because they didn't want them. They couldn't, and they had been searching for answers, undergoing treatments. Robyn had taught on the reservation while they waited for their own children. Then, without warning, she was gone in the blink of an eye, in a single-car accident on her way home from work.

Adam closed his eyes for a moment. But he opened them as quickly as he'd closed them. He couldn't take the images that came in the darkness. That night at the hospital, Jack, his face twisted with grief, the loss of Robyn so great that Adam had almost been surprised when Jack had gone on living.

By Christmas last year, Jack was back at

his practice. He was doing what he'd always done, but the old Jack was gone, and the new Jack, left in his place, seemed numb and lost. On that Christmas, Gage and Adam had both been home, and they'd both told Jack that all he had to do was call, and they'd be back in Wolf Lake for him. He'd never called them on that promise. He never would. But Adam was calling himself on it now.

"There's no time limit on grieving," John said, snapping Adam away from the past.

"I know." But he didn't know at all. He'd been told that by others, as the only major loss in his life, his grandfather, made sense. His grandfather had lived eighty-four years before quietly leaving in his sleep three years ago. He missed the man so much, but he'd had a wonderful life. Robyn's death made no sense to him at all—she'd been barely thirty with her whole life ahead of her. Adam had no idea about the hurt that Jack experienced.

"He's lost, Adam. He's breathing and walking and talking and even working some, but he's not living." Adam felt John's eyes on him as he asked, "So you're going back to do what?"

He didn't know. He only knew he had to

be there. "I'll know that when I see Jack," he replied honestly.

"I think when we get there, we should get Jack to come hunting or fishing or just plain old camping with us, maybe Moses, too, up in the high country where we used to go as kids."

Adam agreed. The five of them—Jack, Gage, Moses, John and himself—had been inseparable when they were young. Now Moses Blackstar was the head of the local hospital, the driving force behind it being built and the one who kept it going. "Getting away from everything, maybe we can talk how we used to back in the day."

"He's turned down Moses's invitations right along," John said, "But if all of us do it, it could happen. It's worth a try." Without warning, John pulled off the highway and into the parking lot for a fast-food place next to a motel and gas station. "I'm hungry," he said. "We can sit and talk for a bit, maybe make some plans, get them in place, then speak to Jack."

Adam didn't want to stop anywhere. He wanted to be in Wolf Lake. "Get it to go, and we can talk while you drive," he said.

He wasn't even sure he could eat right then. His stomach had tightened painfully at the idea of what he'd find when he got home and saw Jack. He wasn't at all certain what that would be. Not at all.

FAITH WAS EXHAUSTED. She'd been on the road for two weeks, stopping at motels in Kentucky, Tennessee, Arkansas and Texas as she traveled south, then west. Her plan had been to keep moving, spend a day or two in each place, nowhere too long, and go through the files when she could. She read and read, hoping to find something that wasn't right. Something that might prove her father was innocent. Anything the others had missed.

But thus far, there had been nothing like that. So she just kept moving. At the moment, she was moving west on Highway 40 toward Albuquerque. She'd made the news quite regularly as a tagline to her father's problems. One headline read Faith Sizemore Stays Out of Sight. It was another, though, that actually hit her the hardest. Sizemore's Daughter Hiding—Subpoena for Grand Jury Fails. Below that, the story began, "While Federal investigators search her home again, Faith Sizemore is nowhere to be seen. An attempt to serve a subpoena for her testimony in front of the grand jury failed and prosecutors say they will keep trying, believing that her testimony could be vital to their case." Did they know she'd run, or did they think she was just "secured" somewhere?

Her stomach grumbled, and at the same time, weariness almost overtook her. She realized she hadn't eaten since breakfast, and she couldn't remember when she'd actually slept for a good number of hours. She covered a yawn, cupped the back of her neck with one hand to knead at the tension. She was exhausted to the point she couldn't concentrate. To keep herself going and to be of any use when reviewing those files, she had to have food, then rest. Real rest.

Peace and privacy for a week was what she needed. But where would she find that? The motels she'd been staying at were not exactly calm and quiet with people coming and going at all hours. And a hotel that would give her peace wouldn't give her privacy, since she couldn't use a credit card.

She rotated her head from side to side to ease the cramping in her muscles and felt as if she hadn't taken an easy breath since leaving Chicago. Looking ahead, she saw a sign that towered into the graying sky, which was rapidly filling with dark clouds. Multicolored neon lights flashed *Willie G's Diner. The best food in town.*

She almost smiled at that as she headed to the exit. The "town" was little more than a gas station, a tepee-shaped souvenir shop with a heavy emphasis on Native American and Western collectibles, and a cluster of trailers beyond the parking lot for the old adobe building that was Willie G's Diner.

She slowed as she spotted a sign on a power pole near the diner's entrance advertising The Wolf Lake Inn. The words were printed over a sepia depiction of what looked like a wolf baying at a crescent moon. But it was the last line that got her full attention: "As much or as little peace and quiet as you want. Rooms by the day or by the week. Come visit us at The Inn."

She took the time to jot down a phone number and address from the sign before parking in front of Willie G's. The building was low-roofed, with faded pinkish-beige walls that were chipped in spots to reveal adobe bricks underneath. Every arched window along the front held a wreath made out of sticks with twinkling lights threaded through them. The lot was barely full, with only four other cars, an 18-wheeler and an old motorcycle.

Faith sat for a long moment after she turned off the engine, fighting the urge to call her father, to hear his voice and feel as if she wasn't totally alone. She had only called him twice from a throwaway cell, and each time, she'd been afraid to speak too long or to be too honest. She hadn't wanted him to hear any fear or worry in her tone and she couldn't bear to hear the somber resignation in his voice. She left the phone alone and got out into the snow and wind to hurry to the entrance. Pushing the door aside, she stepped into comforting warmth, enhanced by the fragrance of food being cooked and woodsmoke that came from a funnel-shaped fireplace set in the middle of the dining area.

The interior echoed the exterior character of the building. Rough, oxidized plaster walls, a ceiling with massive beams made from stripped timber. Well-worn stones underfoot were faded and chipped from years of use. Straight ahead was a counter and beyond that, swinging doors leading to the kitchen.

Booths lined the wall to the right and across the front by the windows, separated only by a large Christmas tree, fully decorated in silver and gold. Wooden tables were arranged in the middle of the room to take advantage of the fireplace. A young girl with brilliant red hair was serving two men at the counter. She looked up as the door thudded shut. "Sit anywhere you'd like," she said with a smile. "I'll be right there."

Christmas music with a definite Western twang played in the background, blending with the customers' conversations. Faith chose a booth by one of the windows. She sank down onto the dark red vinyl bench seat, slipped off her jacket and thought about the sign for the Wolf Lake Inn. "As much or as little Peace and Quiet as you want." She craved both the way a man lost in the desert craved water.

The girl from the counter came over to her and smiled. "Welcome to Willie G's. What will you be having today?" Faith ordered coffee and a hamburger with fries, then sat back as the girl took off for the kitchen.

When the hamburger and stack of fries, both large enough to feed a small nation, came, she knew that she'd made a decision. She was going to find Wolf Lake Inn and stay put for a few days if it looked okay. And she could sleep, really sleep, so she could think straight. She was afraid of making a mistake and being recognized.

She ate half of her food. Pushing aside the plate, she reached for her wallet. She needed to get going.

"Food no good, lady?"

The blunt question startled Faith, and she looked up to find an older man standing by the booth. He was in his middle to late sixties, with weathered skin and long white hair piled under a cook's hairnet. Wearing a white T-shirt and white pants, both liberally stained by various foods, he frowned at her plate, his hawkish nose twitching. "No good?" he repeated as he met her gaze.

She shook her head. "Oh, no, it was very good. It's just so much food, enough for two or three meals."

He folded his arms on his chest as a smile softened his lined, angular face. "I understand. You're a little bit of a thing. For a minute I thought old Willie G. had lost the magic touch."

"What I could eat was great." She couldn't stop a yawn. "Sorry," she said. "I've been driving forever and I'm really tired."

"Where you heading for?"

She hesitated, wondering if he could help. "Albuquerque, but I saw a sign for The Wolf Lake Inn when I pulled in here. Do you know it?"

"You looking to stay there?"

"Maybe, as long as it's peaceful and private, and not too fancy or expensive."

"That about describes it," Willie said

"Is it very far from here?"

"It's about fifteen miles north, near the res."

"The res?"

"Indian reservation."

Faith hadn't realized until that moment that he was very much a Native American. "You're from there?"

He nodded. "Born and bred. Wolf Lake is a good place. Some tourist stuff, but nothing too crazy. It's pretty quiet most times. Shoot, they got a police force of four, and their main job is giving out tickets for illegal parking to tourists who wander through. That tells you how safe it is."

It didn't sound as if any of the four policemen would be looking for a financier's daughter or even know about her. "How do I get there?"

He gave her directions, telling her to watch out for the inn just before the general store on the main drag of the town on the north side. "It's a two-storied adobe with a carved eagle above the entrance. It was the first hotel ever in town. Now it's more like what do you call those places…oh, yeah, a bed-and-breakfast. Six, eight rooms, nice place." He hesitated and then said, "For the sake of truth in advertising, I should tell you my niece runs the inn. Name's Mallory Sanchez. You can tell her I sent you, if you want." He smiled slyly at her. "Probably won't help you, but who knows?"

She answered his smile. "Thank you so much, Mr.…?"

"Name's Willie G. Lots of Willies around, but only one Willie G. in these parts."

The waitress called out to him, "Got two orders, Willie."

He waved a hand at her but didn't turn. "What's your name?"

"Faith."

"Safe journey, Faith," he said, moving toward the kitchen.

After the waitress boxed Faith's leftover food and took the money for the bill, Faith stepped out into air that was just plain cold. Light snow was falling, gradually turning the land a pale gray-white. Faith got in her car, went back to the frontage road and headed east for two miles, then spotted the turn Willie had told her about. She drove onto the narrow two-lane road that was all but deserted in the early evening.

As she drove, there were fewer and fewer houses and buildings. The road cut through a vast desert area, with lots of rocks and rough ground, etched in white. Shadows fell on the snow from the mesas and buttes that rose in erratic patterns.The country looked bleak.

She clicked on her headlights and kept going. Had Willie told her the right distance to Wolf Lake? She felt as if she'd been driving for a lot more time than it took to go fifteen miles. Relief came when she caught sight of a road sign: Wolf Lake—2 Miles.

She sped up, anxious to get there before the dark descended completely.

She was so intent on her driving, she didn't notice she wasn't alone on the road until the jolting wail of a siren cut through the air. Flashing red and blue lights bounced around in the interior of her car. She reflexively glanced at the speedometer, actually happy to see she was speeding. Simple speeding, stupid of her to do it, but this was not about her fleeing Chicago, just her driving.

She took a shaky breath as she pulled onto the shoulder of the road and stopped. It was okay, she told herself. She had the license her dad had given her. When she jumped at the flood of bright light from inside the police car, she admitted that no matter what logic told her, she was afraid.

CHAPTER THREE

JOHN MUTTERED, "Crazy people," when the speeding car came to a full stop. "Thought we'd get this type on the weekend or closer to Christmas when the tourists come around to visit," John grumbled. He tucked the cruiser in behind the compact car with an Illinois plate on it.

There was a single passenger from what Adam could see, a woman grimacing at the glaring light that John had switched on. She wasn't moving at all.

John tipped open the onboard computer, brought it up and put in the license-plate number. A moment later, he was reading the screen. "Gerald Lewis Reich and Martha Reich, Chicago area. Looks like Martha is on her own. Car's clean, and they're clean. Not even a traffic ticket between them in the past five years." He reached for the door handle. "Be right back," he said and got out.

The wind was picking up, swirling the snow, and John ducked his head while he gripped his cap with his free hand. He got to the driver's window as it slowly slid down and he leaned in to speak to the driver. A hand pushed some folded papers out toward John, who took them and stood to read. Then John turned his head as if he was trying to hit his left shoulder with his chin.

Adam knew John was in full uniform and his two-way radio was wired into the shoulder. He spoke into it, then went back to the car. He pushed the papers back to the driver, bent to say something, then jogged back to the cruiser. He slammed the door on the cold wind and snow outside. "Got a call," he said. "It's Amos Joe and Birdie. They're at it again. Got to get there before someone does something stupid again."

He punched the gas on the idling cruiser, veering out and around the car still ahead of them. Adam glanced at the driver, who still had the window partially down. He caught a glimpse of a shadowy shape before they raced past and down the highway. "What about the stop?" Adam asked, motioning behind them.

"She just bought the car and didn't get it registered before she took off, so I let her go."

Adam saw the way John was biting his lower lip and he knew there was more. "What else?"

John shook his head. "Just a hunch, that's all."

"Just a hunch?" he repeated to his friend. "A hunch about what?"

John frowned at the road ahead. "Actually, the thing is, I get a feeling she's scared of something, and not just of a speeding ticket." He shrugged on a gruff laugh. "If I had a dollar for every right hunch I had about people, I'd still be broke."

Adam stared at the darkness outside. "I don't know. Your hunches have worked out sometimes."

"Dumb luck," John muttered.

Maybe John was right about the woman, maybe something was going on, but it wasn't something either man could do a thing about. What they could do was help his brother. "When did you see Jack last?"

John cleared his throat. "Out at your pa's

place." He was referring to Adam's grandfather's ranch just north of their parents' spread.

"Why there?"

"Don't know. Maureen said he'd headed out there, so I followed." Maureen Cane, Jack's assistant in the law office, kept close track of her boss. "I caught up with him sitting on the porch of the old house."

Adam thought maybe the old place gave his brother some comfort. That adobe had been the first thing his grandfather had built when he'd migrated from the high country on the res, down to the low country. Eventually, he brought his expanding family to the raw land that had been in the Wolf family for what seemed forever. Pa, as the boys called their grandfather, had been obsessed all his life about making something out of nothing for his family. He'd been told to stay with his people, to not go off on his own to mingle with others.

But Jackson Wolf, whom Jack had been named for, hadn't listened. He'd followed his own vision. He'd gone down and worked hard and long, clearing first the homesite, building the sprawling adobe to house his seven children, then went on to clear pastures to graze cattle and sheep. When he'd finished, his family had a home with efficiently run land that extended over three hundred acres.

Adam's mother, Lark, had loved it, and when she'd married Herbert Carson, an Irish banker from Boston, whom she'd met by chance in the town, there was no question that they would settle on Wolf land. And they did. They moved south of the original house, onto a piece of land that was three times as big and ended up being three times as fancy.

But the Carson boys had always been drawn to Pa's land. Like metal to a magnet, when school let out and they were free for the summer, they were at the old ranch. They'd trail after their grandfather, working alongside him and listening to his stories about their ancestors and his plans for the land. He'd gone even farther and helped develop the town of Wolf Lake. He'd been there when the name of his people had been put on the town. He'd realized his dreams.

As the squad car drove through the persistent snow, Adam remembered an incident when he'd been around fourteen. The brothers had left Pa's place and hiked up into the fringes of the high country. At sunset, they'd been sitting on a ledge that looked down on the reservation in one direction, the town in the other and the vast expanse of Wolf land far below. Off in the distance, the soaring mountains beyond the buttes and mesas stood starkly against the early-evening sky. A deep gouge that cut through them opened a way to the other side.

Jack had said something about the new grazing area Pa had cleared, that he'd hoped he'd go farther south. Land had always been Jack's passion, the Wolf land. Gage had pointed to a site on the far end of town, to the start of construction for a fully equipped medical clinic that Moses's father would run for years before his son pushed for a real hospital. Gage had said they needed to make it bigger, and they had done that years later, turning it from a clinic to a hospital.

But Adam had looked past the town and the res and over to the separation in the mountains. All he remembered feeling at that moment had been an overwhelming urge to head for the opening and keep going. He wasn't sure where to, but he knew he wanted to go.

Like Pa, he'd wanted to break free.

"We should discuss our trip and have things organized when we talk to Jack," John said, snapping Adam back to the present.

"Good idea. We can contact Moses tomorrow and see if he can get away. It's been a long time since we all went up there together."

John nodded. "Just have to convince Jack to come."

Adam relished watching the town of Wolf Lake rapidly come into sight. The familiar shapes and layout welcomed him yet brought a sense of unease about what he'd find there. It didn't make sense, and when John pulled into the trailer park to find Amos Joe and Birdie, he pushed it out of his mind completely.

FAITH SHIVERED UNEXPECTEDLY despite the warmth in the car, and for a moment, she felt light-headed. Slowing, she opened the window a crack, letting in frigid air and some errant snowflakes. The coolness on her face helped her to settle down a bit. Obviously she wasn't meant for a life of crime. She'd barely been able to nod when the cop who had stopped her had let her off with a stern warning. *Slow down and enjoy the beautiful country,* he'd said.

She kept going, staying below the speed limit, and finally spotted the sign for Wolf Lake. A glow began to spread in the distance ahead. As she got closer, the glow gradually turned into a sprawling town that flowed away from the main highway. She caught the turnoff and found herself driving past small houses, then was jarred when she saw the police cruiser with its lights flashing, parked by some ancient trailers to one side of the road.

She drove past slowly, keeping her eyes on the road. The main street of Wolf Lake was an eclectic mixture of adobe structures, wood frames and brick buildings, all reflecting the reds and greens of Christmas lights. Decorations filled the windows of stores and homes and were strung over the street and outlined most roofs along the way. The whole thing was a merging of the Old West and Native American heritage, overlaid by tons of Christmas cheer. Raised wooden walkways that spoke of the past, when streets turned to mud and snakes could be anywhere, led the route.

Souvenir shops mingled with businesses that ranged from a grocer's to a surveyor's office, a potter's store and a feed-and-tack barn set up in a huge wooden building fronted by haystacks. Native American influences were everywhere, and life-size carvings of wolves framed several doorways.

She spotted a few restaurants, then finally saw what she was looking for, The Wolf Lake Inn. It was what Willie G. had described, a well-kept two-story, flat-fronted adobe structure set well back from the street behind a low stone fence. A carving of an eagle in flight hung over the entrance, faded with age and layered with pure white snow. A red neon sign flashed *Vacancy* in one of the six arched windows on either side of a broad stoop and a heavy wooden front door.

Faith was excited as she pulled into one of the parking spots outside the fence. Only one other car was there, a blue van with a bumper sticker that read California or Bust. She got out, grabbed her purse and hurried to the door. There was a huge knocker fashioned like a wolf's head, with its onyx eyes staring out at the night. She ignored it and pushed the door open. A low chime rang somewhere inside.

The front of the first floor was used for a large reception and sitting area, split by a staircase that led up to the second level. Dark wood and lovely furnishings made for a warm, cozy atmosphere. A huge Christmas tree stood to one side of the stairs, its lights twinkling with turquoise and silver decorations. Rugs in rich earth tones partially covered tiles that were worn and faded to a reddish-brown.

"Hello there," a voice said, drawing Faith's attention to the reception desk that ran along the left wall and was backed by an old-fashioned cubby for letters. A swinging door by the cubby was still moving as a lithe, black-haired lady came up behind the desk flashing a brilliant smile. Narrowed eyes assessed Faith. "So you did decide to come," the woman said.

"I'm sorry?" Faith asked, approaching the desk.

"Willie G. said you might be coming by." She held out her hand and introduced herself. "I'm Mallory Sanchez and I'm guessing you're Faith." Her black hair was straight and fell loosely to her waist. Chocolate-brown eyes were warm against a creamy tan, and jeans worn with a heavy red sweater showed off her slender frame. A pretty woman by any standards, and her smile made her even more attractive.

"Faith Arden," Faith said, taking the woman's hand when she offered it and met a surprisingly firm grip. "I didn't expect Willie to call you about me."

"He was calling about something else, a big Christmas party, actually, but mentioned you might be coming by. He said you're looking for a place to rest."

Faith felt uneasy at her words. The police stop had been bad enough. She didn't want to be a topic of conversation for the town. "I need a room," she said with more coolness than she intended.

"Well, of course you do," Mallory said and spun an old registration book around to face her, then handed Faith a pen with a bobbing Santa head on the end of it. "Just put in your information, and let me see your identification."

Faith handed the fake driver's license to

Mallory, who said, "The inn is peaceful and you can get a good rest here. No problem."

"That's great," Faith murmured while she quickly signed her name, then stopped. She was drawing a blank for her address. What was wrong with her? She'd used that address in Rockford at every stop so far, but she couldn't for the life of her recall it right then.

Mallory asked, "Is there a problem?"

"Oh, no, I'm just so tired," she said and yawned without having to force it. Then the address came to her and she quickly wrote it on the ledger. "I've been driving forever."

Mallory glanced at the information in the book, made a notation off her driver's license, then handed it back to Faith. "I hope you didn't drive all the way from Illinois nonstop?" She smiled at the absurdity of her question and didn't wait for Faith to answer. "Do you want the first or second floor? Although, if you're here to rest and take it easy, the second floor is probably your best bet. It's more private, and there's only one guest up there in a front room, a gentleman from Texas."

"That sounds good, second floor, in the back?"

"We have a great room at the end of the hallway with its own bathroom. The other rooms up there have to share. It's a bit more, of course, but it's very nice."

When she mentioned the daily rate, Faith was okay with it, and although she doubted she'd stay more than a few days, she asked about the weekly rate. The figure was 20 percent less than the daily. "I'll take it for two nights," Faith said and paid for the room. When Mallory argued she should see the room first, Faith wanted to say, *If it has a bed and a door to lock, I'm sold,* but instead said, "I'm sure it will be fine."

Mallory selected one of the keys from the cubby and talked as she led the way to the staircase. "We have more choices if you need to change. We have two rooms down and four rooms up." Faith followed her up the stairs onto a small landing that branched out in either direction. They went left and passed only one door as they walked toward the end of the corridor.

Mallory unlocked the door to Faith's room, flipped on a light, then stepped aside for Faith to go in first. "If this doesn't work for you, I have another that might do."

Faith barely heard Mallory. The room was perfect. A huge poster bed fashioned out of what looked like stripped tree trunks stood by a window framed by lace curtains. The floor, worn wooden planks, was warmed by a braided rug in blues and lavenders that matched the bedding. An open door to the right exposed a small bathroom, and a closet on the opposite wall stood open and empty.

"What do you think?" Mallory asked as Faith went to the window and looked down at a garden area dominated by a leafless tree that was almost as tall as the building itself. Snow covered the ground and chairs were tipped up on three tables. It looked right. No one would be out there in this weather.

Faith could almost feel the knots in her body starting to dissolve. "This is fine," she replied. Mallory crossed to a large armoire by the bathroom door and opened both doors. A TV sat on a top shelf over another shelf that flipped forward to make a writing desk. Faith had to fight the urge to just collapse on the big bed.

"Why don't we go down for your things, then you can settle in and get your rest?"

Five minutes later, Faith had her bag and

computer in the room and she was closing the door behind her and locking it. While she'd retrieved her things from the car, Mallory had put a pitcher of ice water along with a glass on a tray by the bed. A chocolate mint lay on the fluffy pillows piled against the headboard, and the scent of roses faintly drifted on the warm air.

Faith felt weariness wash over her. She sank down onto the bed, tugged off her boots and pushed back until she was half sitting against the pillows. The chocolate fell to one side and slid to the floor, but she didn't pick it up. She thought she'd rest for a few minutes, then set up the computer on the desk and pull up the files.

The next thing Faith knew, she woke with a start, and for a second she couldn't remember where she was, but then the world settled. One look at the bedside clock showed her she'd been asleep for over two hours. It was almost eight o'clock. She got off the bed, stretching her hands over her head. Should she just go to her car and get the leftovers she had from Willie G.'s place or see if there was someplace close by to get something hot to eat?

She tugged on her boots, grabbed her jacket, her car keys and wallet, then went downstairs. A man and woman were relaxing in front of the fireplace. On the table in front of them were wineglasses, a carafe of deep red wine, and a platter of crackers, meat and cheese.

If things had been normal, she would have said hello to the couple, filled a plate with cheese and crackers, poured a glass of wine and gone back up stairs. But since she'd left Chicago, she hadn't been normal. She stayed away from people as much as possible to avoid contact, hopefully without looking odd or being remembered by any of them.

No one was behind the reception desk, so she avoided seeing the owner. She quietly passed behind the couple, reached the door and cringed at the soft chime that sounded when she opened it. She quickly slipped out into the biting cold.

She got into her car, started the engine and the heater, then put her things on the passenger seat and let herself relax for a moment. Slowly, she backed out onto the street and turned away from the direction she'd entered the town. She drove along the deserted street and spotted a modest shop that was open. Its neon light proclaimed it as The Hitching Post, along with advertisements for sandwiches, burgers, cold drinks and doughnuts. A real mixture of offerings, she thought as she stopped her car in front of the low brick structure.

The snow had let up a bit, she noted as she left her car and sprinted into the store. She got a sandwich, some cookies and a take-out cup of coffee. When she reached her car, her attention was drawn by raised voices close by.

"Jack!" a male voice ordered. "We have to talk this over."

She glanced over and saw two men nearby on the sidewalk. One had his back to her. He was at least six feet or more, with broad shoulders that tested the seams of a leather jacket trimmed in shirred wool that he wore with jeans and black cowboy boots. She took in the sound of his quick breathing as he faced the other man.

Faith couldn't see that man's face, since it was lost in the shadows and he had a cap pulled low on his face. He was in a blue down jacket with dark pants and running shoes. She couldn't see his expression, but she didn't miss the edge to his voice when he countered, "Leave me alone! I am not a charity case, and I don't need you suggesting—"

"Hey, I'm not here for charity," the first man said in a lower, calmer voice. "I came because—"

The man in the cap spun on his heel and hurried off with a wave of one hand over his shoulder. "Go back to where you came from," he said as he strode off down the sidewalk.

Faith realized she'd been eavesdropping and quickly went to open her car door. But before she could escape, the remaining man turned abruptly and ran right into her. Her coffee flew out of her hand, and her bag of food fell at her feet along with her wallet and keys.

She bent quickly to gather what she could, and the man did the same, his large hand grabbing her bag while she got the rest. "I'm really sorry," he said as they crouched and faced each other.

She looked up into a face with sharp features, a strong jaw that showed a new beard, then eyes as dark as the night around them.

She felt flustered under his intent gaze and stood. He matched her action and seemed to tower over her. “I…I wasn’t looking where I was going,” she said in a breathless voice. “I’m sorry.” She looked away from the man, her gaze landing on her coffee, which had spilled right by her car. “Oh, shoot.”

“What were you drinking?” the stranger asked.

“Just plain old coffee,” she muttered, frowning at the still spreading pool of brown liquid that was melting the snow beneath it.

Before she realized what he was doing, the stranger had gone into the shop. She could guess what he was up to, and soon he returned with a cup in his hand, which he held out to her. “My treat,” he said with a smile that revealed a dimple on his right cheek.

“Oh, no,” she said, awkwardly trying to get her wallet open.

“I mean it,” he stated firmly. “I was distracted by…” He shrugged, his smile fading. “I feel it’s my duty to make sure a visitor’s stay in Wolf Lake is a pleasant one.”

She was thankful her mouth didn’t drop open with surprise that he’d spotted her as a visitor so easily. "How would you know that?"

"Easy," he said and that dimple was gone.

Faith felt her anxiety rising. Enough was enough. She quickly took the coffee he offered her, ignoring the warm touch of his hand, and said, "Thank you."

He inclined his head slightly, looked past her and his brows knit together questioningly. She turned to see he was checking out her car. "You're from Illinois?"

She nodded as she opened the car door and slipped inside. She set her things down, wanting to close the door, but the man was still there, blocking her. "Yes, from Illinois."

"You're a long way from home," he said.

In that moment, she felt intensely her total isolation, and she almost hated him for saying it out loud to her. "A long way," she echoed.

He had his hand on the top of the door frame. "I'm Adam," he said, expecting her to give him her name, but she didn't.

"And you live here," she finished for him.

"Used to. Right now I'm just home for Christmas."

He wasn't aware of her situation, thankfully, but everything he said made her feel sad. He was home for Christmas, and she knew she wouldn't be. She wouldn't be home for her birthday or New Year's Eve, and probably not for a long while. She felt the heat of tears stinging her eyes and quickly said her thanks.

He drew back, and she slammed the door shut with more force than she intended to. Without looking at him again, she pulled onto the street and drove back to the inn. She was worse off than she thought she was if a total stranger could make her feel this way just by making innocent conversation. She really needed to relax and calm down for more than a few days.

But she couldn't and she hated that. The tears came silently. She hated tears, too, but couldn't stop them, either. Like so much else in her life…

CHAPTER FOUR

ADAM WATCHED THE WOMAN with the soft dark curls, amazing blue eyes and a voice that was slightly breathless drive away and he felt stunned. First by her, then by the car she was driving.

When he'd turned into her, so angry at Jack that he could barely see straight, he'd stopped dead. In front of him was a woman with delicate features, incredible eyes and a creamy complexion. He had to admit that just then he'd all but forgotten about Jack.

Their fight was nothing new. His brother had always been stubborn, not one to accept help, and Adam had figured out ages ago that going head-to-head with him was a mistake. But he'd forgotten that earlier and regretted it now. He'd try again. He wasn't giving up, nor was he going to give up on the small but smart-looking woman he'd towered over.

Tiny but resolute when she'd tried to refuse that replacement cup of coffee. And even when he'd persisted and won, he hadn't felt he'd had a victory as much as she'd allowed him to do it to stop any argument.

Then the car. The blue compact with Illinois plates on it. The same car John had stopped on the road to Wolf Lake. John had had a feeling about her, a hunch, and Adam had seen something himself in her expression. It wasn't really fear, maybe anxiousness—something he was having a hard time defining anyway. Uncertainty, impatience? He could usually read people quite easily, but not her.

He finally headed down the street toward where he'd parked his truck and gone looking for Jack. He pushed his hands into his pockets and hunched into the wind. The blue car was gone, the red taillights swallowed up by the night. Running into that woman had cut through his frustration with Jack, easing it briefly, but now it was back. He loved his brother, but his resistance had stunned him. No, he didn't understand losing someone like that, but he wanted to help and he would.

He got to his truck, climbed in and went

directly to the family ranch, where he was staying in the guesthouse. "Welcome home," he said to the emptiness around him. He had the crazy image of a woman waiting there to greet him; she had dark curls and a smile he wished he hadn't seen. "Stupid," he muttered, but that didn't blot out the memory of those blue eyes.

INCREDIBLY, FAITH SLEPT well that night, no dreams, no nervously waking only to realize that no one was pounding on her door wanting to arrest her. It was just past eight, and she got up right away, dressed and glanced at the paper sack that still held the untouched sandwich from the night before.

She felt better, and she had a feeling it was time to just go and not stay a second day. Wolf Lake was nice but so small, and she knew she'd be conspicuous. The man the night before had spotted her for a visitor, and others would, too. The visitor who wasn't doing any sightseeing, she thought and knew it was time to drive on.

She got her things together and arrived at the registration desk an hour later. The couple from the night before were helping themselves to coffee and Danish pastries. Mallory was behind the desk.

"Good morning," the woman said, eyeing Faith's bags in either hand. "You're not leaving, are you?"

"Yes, I need to check out."

Mallory frowned with concern. "You aren't happy with the room? I told you, I could move you—"

"No, it's not that. I had a good rest and really need to get on the road again."

"Oh, okay," she said, then her smile flashed. "Well, if you're ever near Wolf Lake again, come on back and stay a bit longer." She counted out Faith's refund for the unused second night.

Faith wished she could stay, but she knew she'd never be back to this town. "Thanks," she said again, collecting her things and heading for the door.

The morning was gray and cold. Snow from the night before covered everything, and only a couple of cars were driving down the recently plowed street. She spotted patches of ice on the black asphalt.

The interior of her car was freezing. Quickly, she pushed the key into the ignition. The engine turned over and she flipped on the heater. She was thinking about heading north to Colorado as she reached for the gearshift. Everything came to a stop as she caught a whiff of something burning followed by a sudden sputter of the engine right before it died. She stared at the gauges, saw a check-engine light was on and noticed the acrid smell in the air.

This couldn't be happening. This car was everything to her. She couldn't rent one and risk leaving a trail for the authorities to find. There was no bus or train service handy. And she couldn't walk. The best-laid plans never worked out, Faith thought, trying the key again. Nothing. Not even a click.

The temperature was bitter cold. She just shook her head. So many things she hadn't taken into consideration. The car was used. Because it had been running so well for the past two weeks, the thought of it breaking down hadn't even entered her mind.

She grabbed her wallet and got out of the car, locking it. It took a full second before she realized she'd just left her keys in the ignition. She wanted to scream or maybe laugh at the absurdity of the moment. Instead, she made herself breathe evenly and think. A mechanic. Surely Wolf Lake had an auto repair shop somewhere.

With a heavy sigh, she returned to the inn. Mallory was still behind the registration desk. She looked up as the chime sounded and saw Faith. "Hey, did you forget something?" she began, then her smile faltered as she saw Faith's expression. "What's wrong?" she asked, quickly coming around the desk.

"My car won't start. I just wanted to know where I can find a mechanic."

"Sure, of course. Just farther down the street." She motioned to the west. "Manaw's Garage is on the other side of the street, three or four blocks down." She gestured at the phone on the desk. "Let me call him," she said, reaching for the receiver.

"Oh, no," Faith said quickly. She didn't want the woman involved any more than she already was. "I can walk down there."

Mallory hesitated. "You sure?"

"Absolutely. I appreciate the offer, though," she said to soften her refusal. "I'll get going."

Mallory called after her, "Ask for Dent."

Faith waved a hand and stepped back outside. She got to the street, headed west, and after a couple of blocks, she spotted her target. She crossed the street and arrived at Manaw's Garage.

The building looked old and settled, with none of the cuteness of faux adobe or Old West touches. It was weathered wood and stone, with twin gas pumps standing by the street in front of the two service bays. As she approached the closest one, she spotted the mechanic, a short, stocky man with a shaved head wearing an oil-stained denim jacket over equally stained orange overalls.

He stood under an ancient truck raised on a lift and turned when her boots hit the cement floor with a dull thud. He came out from under the truck and smiled. "How's it going, little lady?"

Little lady? She almost smiled at that. Wolf Lake could be quaint. "My car broke down. The battery, I think. It won't start."

"The make and year?"

She told him and finished with, "It's over at—"

"The Inn. I know," he said, rubbing his dirty hands on a soiled rag.

"How did—"

"I know?" he asked for her. "Saw the car

there this morning. Always notice a new car in town. Assumed you were staying there."

Faith was grateful she could dismiss the irritation she'd felt thinking Mallory had called after she'd asked her not to. Faith guessed everyone that lived here pretty much knew everything going on. "Well, it's there, and I accidently locked the keys in it."

He grinned. "I can get in any car in less than a minute," he assured her, and she wondered if that was a good thing. "I'll be over there in an hour or so."

"How long do you think it will take to fix it?"

"No way to tell until I get a look-see at the problem. If it's a battery, no time. Be done today. But if it's more, I don't know. Depends on what and how bad it is. Just give me a number to reach you at, and I'll be in touch as soon as I figure it out."

Her heart sank. She didn't want to give out the number of the pay-as-you-go cell she'd bought before leaving Texas. No one had that number. Then she knew what she'd have to do, at least for the next few hours. "I'm at the inn, so you can call there." She would check with Mallory during the day.

"Great."

"Thank you, sir," she said.

"I'm no sir. I'm Denton Manaw, sole owner and head mechanic at this establishment. But people call me Dent."

"Dent," she repeated. "I'm Faith. And thank you again."

He nodded, then got back to work on the truck.

She walked away slowly, toward the inn, taking her time, checking out the town. Wolf Lake felt so comfortable, as if it belonged right where it was, as native to the area as the buttes and mesas were. No rush, no fuss, and nice people, if they were like Mallory and Dent. The memory of Adam came to her. He was nice, too, she suspected. He'd bought her another coffee and obviously felt bad about running into her.

She glanced into several windows decked out for Christmas and considered what it would be like to live in a place like this. It was a world away from Chicago in more ways than one. When she spotted the same coffee shop she'd gone to the previous evening, she ducked inside, ordered coffee and a pastry, then took a table by the window that overlooked the street. Slow and easy. It was good to just sit still for a bit. There was nothing else she could do, so she sipped her steaming coffee and nibbled on the flaky pastry.

She hadn't been there more than ten minutes when she looked out the window and spied a tall man striding down the sidewalk. He was heading in her direction. There were the leather jacket, faded jeans and boots she recognized. Adam, she thought, but now he had a dark Stetson pulled low to shadow his face. He walked quickly, an obvious destination in mind, and she wondered if he was searching for the man he'd argued with the night before.

As he got nearer, he glanced up and to his left, then waved to someone across the street and kept walking. As he got closer, she had to fight an impulse to move back from the window. But she stayed put as he came abreast of her on the other side of the glass. She looked down into her coffee, sure that he was going to pass without noticing her. She was wrong.

There was a tap on the window, and she looked up, knowing who she'd see. Adam. His intense gaze was on her, then the smile she'd seen last night, the one dimple exposed by the expression. He looked rugged and confident, as if he fit right in at Wolf Lake. She managed a nod, formed what she hoped was a pleasant smile for him, and all the while her heart was hammering against her ribs.

Please keep walking, she pleaded silently, but he had no intention of going past with a mere wave and a smile. He headed for the shop's entrance, all but dwarfing the space. In a few strides he was at her table. Without hesitating or asking if it was okay, he pulled out a chair and sat across from her, taking off the Stetson and putting in on an empty chair by him.

His eyes flicked to her coffee. "I promise not to get too close to that," he said with that wry grin.

Did the man know what effect he had on women, or was he one of those guys who didn't have a clue? Staring into his dark eyes, she wasn't sure. His smile was genuine, his body language showed ease, and if he smiled fully again, she wasn't sure what she'd do. But she knew she wasn't going to drink any more coffee. She kept her hands clasped in her lap under the table.

He glanced out the window, then back at her. "So how's it going for you in Wolf Lake?"

"Good," she said tentatively, "although I really haven't seen much of what's around here."

His gaze held hers and that made her even more nervous. "Maybe you need a tour guide," he said, one dark eyebrow lifted slightly.

Darn, he was… She erased that image, knowing any thoughts about him being sexy were out of order, especially given the circumstances. "No, I'm leaving today." She hoped that was the truth. "I'm just getting a few things done before I go."

For a moment she thought she saw a flash of disappointment in those eyes, but the recovery was so swift, she was sure she'd imagined it. "Well," he murmured, "I hope you get back sometime, and if I'm here…" He shrugged. "Who knows?"

What she knew was that wouldn't happen. That made her feel… She didn't know, but it wasn't pleasant. It was all so bizarre. At any other time, if Adam had sat down across from her, she would have definitely talked with him, got to know him a bit, to maybe let whatever he was hinting at blossom, but that was out of the question. "Who knows?" she repeated softly.

He frowned, his head tipped slightly to one side as if considering something. He leaned forward, his forearms on the table, his strong hands clasped together. He paused before he finally spoke again. "You know, to be honest, I've got the feeling that I'm a problem for you." The smile was gone completely now.

Shock zinged through her, and she didn't know what to say. A problem? "What?"

"Maybe not a problem, but I'm making you upset and I'm sorry for that." She had a heart-stopping moment when his hand moved and she thought he was going to reach out and make contact with her. Thankfully, he didn't. "I'm going out on a limb here, because I'm not sure what's going on, but if you need help, someone to talk to, I'm a great listener." She wasn't sure what expression she had on her face because he quickly added, "Just someone to *talk* to."

His offer was genuine, she could sense that, and that was what terrified her. He could tell she was alone, that she had no one to confide in and that she would have loved to have that luxury.

What scared her the most was his reading her so perfectly when she'd thought she was being so outwardly contained. "No," she sputtered, her panic rising to the surface. "There's nothing, not anything." She tried to slow herself down, to actually sound as if she were fine. "But it was good meeting you," she said, acknowledging how much she really meant that. She reached for her wallet. "I need to go."

Adam stood, looked down at her, and her knees felt weak. He spoke softly. "Have a good life. Just remember, I'll be coming back here more often now."

"I don't think I'll be back, but if I am..."

"Look for me?" When she didn't answer his question, he added, "There is something that I need to ask you, though."

She braced herself for any lie she had to tell to get out of there. "What's that?"

"Who are you?"

She felt a rush of anxiety flood her senses. "Ex...cuse me?" she managed.

"If I come back, I need to know who to ask about. You never told me your name."

Oh. If she could have done a backflip out of joy at such a simple question, she would have done it. But all she did was take a breath before answering him. "Faith."

"Faith," he murmured, that smile flitting at the corners of his mouth. "Faith."

She nodded and moved past him to get to the door.

She stepped out onto the street, turned abruptly to go and noticed at the first corner she came to that she'd gone in the wrong direction to get to the inn. She could see Manaw's garage two blocks ahead. She felt too unnerved to care at that moment and just kept going until she got to the next corner. She darted a look behind her.

Adam was nowhere to be seen. *Who are you?* he'd asked. The words had contained as much force as a physical punch.

She pulled her jacket more tightly around her, kept going and circled back at the end of the block to pass a mixture of trailers, houses and bare land. Then she took another street that led to the main drag and came out a block beyond the inn.

She glanced up and down the street, and when she didn't see a tall man in a leather jacket and a black Stetson, she rushed as best she could over the frozen snow toward the porch. In the few seconds it took her to get to the inn's door, she realized something had changed. She took in the empty space where her car had been parked.

Dent had come faster than she'd hoped, and she felt a degree of excitement, until she remembered she hadn't only locked her keys in the car. There was also her purse, her computer, her travel bag and everything in the glove compartment, too. She stood very still and fought the urge to scream at the top of her lungs.

ADAM REMAINED AT the coffee shop for a long time, staring at Faith's barely touched pastry and mug of coffee. Faith. He stood slowly, tugged on his Stetson. "So that's that," he breathed to himself as he did up his jacket and headed for the door.

The street was almost deserted in that quiet time between breakfast and lunch. Only a few people were on foot, and not one of them was Faith. Then he saw a police cruiser pull in next to his truck near Jack's office. John got out, his sunglasses firmly in place as he scanned the street, then spotted Adam and waved to him.

Adam jogged over to him as he leaned back against the cruiser, arms crossed on his chest. "Heard you were out and about. I thought your folks would have you tied up with the party preparations."

Adam grinned at the absurdity of John's supposition. The party was, and always would be, entirely his mother's. His father tolerated it, and the boys, who had loved it as kids, only showed up sporadically as adults. But for the first time in a long time, he was almost looking forward to it. "Mom's practically living in the main barn overseeing the staging."

"She loves it," John pointed out. "And my kids are chomping at the bit to get there."

"Where are you heading now?" Adam asked.

"I was looking for you. Your dad said you'd gone to town first thing. Thought I'd find you around here." He inclined his head in the direction of Jack's office.

Adam had come in early for breakfast with an old friend who ran a diner on the far end of town, then he intended to stop by to see Jack and make amends for his words the night before. But between the breakfast and finding Jack, he'd found Faith. "Why were you looking for me?"

"I have something to discuss with you. Didn't want to do it over the phone." His eyes narrowed as he spoke. "Nothing life-and-death, but important."

"What?" Adam asked, curious.

John motioned to the cruiser. "Get in and we'll drive while we talk. An extra patrol car on the streets is a good thing around the holidays."

When John steered the cruiser out onto the street in the direction of the road to the res, Adam finally asked, "What's going on?"

John didn't beat around the bush. "Jack. He called me first thing this morning to let me know he was on his way to the airport because he's leaving for a week or so."

Adam turned and stared at his friend. "What? I was talking to him last night and he didn't mention a thing about going anywhere. In fact, he was saying he had a lot of work coming up and he'd be tied up until after Christmas."

"Well, he got untied," John said in his usual blunt manner.

"Where's he going?"

"Northwest, up to Washington State."

Suddenly, everything made sense to Adam. "He's going to see Robyn's brother?" Robyn had been a twin and she'd been very close to her brother, Robert, even after he'd relocated to the Seattle area a year before Robyn's accident. Robert and his wife had a son, Trace, and Robyn had been crazy about the child. The last time Adam had seen Robert and his wife, Isabel, had been at the funeral.

"Yes," John said, his eyes focused on the street ahead of them. "He said he needs to talk to Robert, and he's got some Christmas gifts for Trace, and he wanted to give them to him personally."

That was all well and good, except that Jack had called John to let him know what he was going to do. Not his family. "Why did he call you?" he asked.

"Didn't say, but my guess is he didn't want an argument."

That made sense after last night. He exhaled and looked out at the passing stores and homes. "Maybe it will help for him to be there," he said, more to himself than to John.

As John replied, "Exactly," Adam's attention was distracted when he spotted a blue car parked about a half block ahead of them. He sat up a bit, then sank back when the plate was in state and not from Illinois. "Problem?" John asked, following his line of sight.

"No, no problem," Adam said. "Just saw a car I thought I recognized." They were passing the hospital and the Family Center next to it, a place that offered help to local children who had special learning or physical needs. But there were no more cars that looked familiar.

"That car you stopped on our way here?" Adam asked.

"What about it?"

"The lady in it?"

John just nodded.

"What was her name?"

John frowned, scratched his chin for a second. "Faith Arden, I think. Why?"

"Address?"

John frowned again. "Why?"

"No reason," he muttered as he adjusted his Stetson.

"Don't remember beyond Illinois," John said.

He almost made a sarcastic comment, but kept it to himself. It wasn't John's fault that the woman was an enigma. It was a fact of life that people often didn't come into your life at the right time. Faith had come into his life abruptly and left just as quickly. It obviously wasn't the right time for her and him. And that was life.

CHAPTER FIVE

FAITH GOT HER THINGS back from Dent soon after he'd taken her car, but two days later she was still stuck in Wolf Lake. She'd been able get the same room at the inn from an obliging Mallory, and she was thankful for it. It was quiet and peaceful, so much so that Faith was consistently sleeping through the night, despite the state of her broken-down car.

Dent was really struggling to figure out why her wiring shorted out and burned through most of the connections. But he was methodically trying to redo the wiring and fix the other problems it had caused.

Still, she was thankful that she had no nightmares to remember, no waking up early, and less and less of that sense of dread that she'd known since leaving Chicago. She stayed in her room most of the time, reading newspapers, watching TV or going through the files. She left for food and for newspapers, and went right back. So far, it had been working out perfectly for her. She hadn't seen Adam again, which she knew she should be grateful for, and she was barely being noticed by the locals. As soon as her car was working again, she'd leave, but until then, she was starting to feel almost safe. She hadn't made the news as anything other than a modifier, as in "the daughter of..."

In jeans, a loose white shirt, her boots, and holding her jacket and wallet, she left for her usual morning coffee and newspapers. When she got back to the inn, Mallory would be there, as she had been the other mornings, and she'd scold Faith for not making use of her continental breakfast. They'd sit and chat a bit before Faith headed back up to her room. They were surprisingly comfortable conversations, pleasant breaks for Faith before she returned to her solitude.

She'd learned quite a bit about Mallory. That they were a year apart in age, Mallory being older, that Mallory had been married but was widowed two years go. She ran the inn pretty much by herself, didn't date at all, thought she never would again and Willie G. was the closest thing she had to a father. He was her uncle on her mother's side. Thankfully, Mallory didn't pump Faith for personal details beyond what she offered.

Fifteen minutes later, she was back at the inn with coffee, pastries and two newspapers. Faith had barely gone inside before a door upstairs opened and closed, and she heard voices. The man from Texas in the room down the hall from hers had been replaced with a couple from Phoenix. Faith retreated into the sitting area as the man and woman came down, talking about getting "a good look at the reservation," and then promptly left.

Faith heard footsteps right before the swinging door behind the counter opened. She turned to smile as Mallory appeared, and for the first time since she'd met the woman, there was no smile in return. Mallory looked upset. "Oh, Faith," she said, "good morning. Sorry, I…got distracted and didn't hear you leave or come back."

Faith wanted to pretend she wasn't aware of her distress, but she couldn't. Mallory was the only person she really spoke to, and she had been more than kind to Faith. "Is there something wrong?"

Mallory shook her head and let out a heavy sigh. "No, not really, but… I don't know."

"Do you want to talk about it?" She couldn't believe she was asking that. The same words from Adam that second day had terrified her, and they jeopardized her firm promise to herself to not get involved. But that didn't stop Faith from motioning to the chairs by the hearth where they usually sat to talk. Mallory nodded and crossed to sink into one of the chairs. Faith put her stuff on the table nearby, then sat and waited.

Mallory seemed to be having difficulty knowing what to say, and Faith gave her time. Then she took a breath and leaned toward Faith slightly. "I'm not sure what to do about something. I'm just confused, and I can't believe that I'm so confused, but I need to talk, if it's okay."

That question was Faith's way out, but as she felt tension start in her neck, she knew she couldn't beg off now. So she sat calmly until a terrible thought struck her. Could Mallory know who she really had as a guest at her inn? Faith had let herself think she was safe here. Maybe she'd been wrong. Her hands were clenched in her lap, and she fought to make the next words sound as casual as possible. "You…can tell me anything," she said, barely controlling her emotions.

When Mallory finally spoke in a rush of words, Faith was shocked at how wrong she'd been. "There's this huge party that a prominent family in town gives every year around Christmas. It's huge. It's in this massive barn that's nicer than some homes, and there's dancing and music and…" She hugged herself and Faith could see she was either shaking or she was shivering. Either way, she seemed unsteady. "I haven't gone for a few years. I…I think I want to go this year—however, I really don't think I should."

Faith was light-headed with relief. "You… you should go, if you want to go."

"I wish it was that simple. I told you about Henry. He's been gone two years now." She shook her head. "We used to go every year, ever since we were kids. But since he passed, I couldn't do it, not by myself. What would people think? That I'm out there having fun and Henry…" She frowned. "Oh, I'm not looking for sympathy. It's just, I want to go, but I feel so guilty. And everyone around here that's my age is married or dating." She crossed and then uncrossed her legs. "I don't want to date or anything. I simply want to go to the party." She looked ready to cry. "But I can't. It's not right, I know that, and I'm being stupid to think about it, but it's Christmas and..." She bit her lip and let the sentence fade.

Faith felt Mallory's sadness like a boulder on her chest. "Surely it would be okay for you to go," she finally said. "You're young, and Henry wouldn't want you to be sad, would he? He loved you, and when you love someone, you want them to be happy, no matter what."

Mallory's eyes welled up. "Henry loved me, and I love him." Faith didn't miss the present tense when Mallory talked about her love for her dead husband. "But I can't do it alone, and there's no one to ask." She flushed slightly. The color in her face deepened and she stood. "I know, I'm babbling. I'm so sorry."

Faith's resolution to keep her distance was crumbling. Bad enough Mallory was widowed, but to not even go to a Christmas party? "You really can't go alone?"

Mallory shook her head. "It's different around here. Everyone grew up together, and most are couples. It's a third-wheel kind of thing, and it makes people uncomfortable. And they all knew Henry. I'm just being silly," she said.

"Where is this place?"

"It's at the Carson ranch, a massive spread just outside of town. The party's in the barn, as I said, and it's like fantasyland come true. Henry used to say it was like visiting the Land of Oz, it was so wonderful. There's a ton of food, and the music is by local bands. The family does this every year for the town—they're such great people." There was a shadow of a smile back on her lips as she got lost in the description. "The kids get gifts and there's entertainment for them, and Santa, of course."

Faith didn't know where it came from, but without giving herself time to think about it too much, she asked, "How long would you stay if you went to the party?"

Mallory seemed confused by the question.

"Well, as long as I wanted to, I guess. I mean, people come and go all evening."

"When is it?"

"Tomorrow evening at six."

Faith wasn't a Good Samaritan, not a rescuer of any sort short of her finding a lost kitten when she was six years old. Her dad had let her keep it, and it had run away a week later. But Mallory seemed more lost than any kitten. "Mallory?" she said, shocked at what she was going to do. "What if I went with you?"

Mallory stared at her. "Are you serious?"

"Yes, my car's still in the garage, but if we can go, have a look around, then leave, it would be okay."

"Oh, yes, yes. I can. We can," she said breathlessly.

Faith stood, wondering what had possessed her to do this. But one look into Mallory's eyes, where hope was starting to grow, told her all she had to know. In and out. Lose herself in the crowd, then leave as soon as she could. "Okay, we have a date." Then she qualified it. "As long as my car's still dead and Dent doesn't have it fixed by then."

The hug was unexpected, but genuine.

Mallory looked ecstatic when she drew back. "Thank you so much." She turned and picked up the items Faith had bought at the store. "I can't believe this," she said on a sigh as she headed upstairs, leading the way to Faith's room. "I mean, this is wonderful. You're wonderful. The party will be wonderful. It's not really fancy at all. Nice jeans and a blouse, or a dress, but nothing too much. If you don't have anything to wear, I'll go shopping with you, if you like?"

Enough was enough. "I've got something to wear, *if* we go," she told her. "Just let me know what time."

"You bet," Mallory said. "It's going to be wonderful." Then she was gone.

"If my car's not ready!" But Mallory never heard those words.

Faith went to the desk and flopped into the chair facing the computer. She had little hope of anything wonderful materializing at a party in a barn surrounded by strangers, but she'd make good on her promise. Still, she chastised herself as she opened her coffee. It was tepid now and not worth drinking. And she was going to a party.

ADAM WAS RIGHT in the middle of the madness. The barn, a network of stalls and tack rooms, all built around an expansive center section sixty feet square, had been transformed with tinsel and lights. A massive Christmas tree, a dance floor with a stage raised for the musicians, and a giant spread of food and drinks completed the picture.

People had been arriving for the past hour, and couples were already dancing. Kids were being entertained by elves and a Santa who looked more like Santa than Santa did. There was laughter and music and good people Adam had known most of his life. He wandered around, speaking to folks and being pleasantly surprised that he was enjoying himself even though, usually, he wasn't a fan of crowds. Until he spotted his mother speaking to some kids near Santa Claus.

That brought Adam up short. He had asked John not to say anything about Jack leaving for Washington State, to let him tell her and his father. She'd been so busy, and he wanted to tell her at the right time. But the moment never seemed to happen. He had to let her know soon. She'd be expecting Jack at the party. He knew he should do it now, but he couldn't, not when his mother was happily greeting another family, the smile on her face radiant. He walked off in the other direction. He'd tell her about Jack soon.

He glanced around at all the people, and yet he had a feeling of isolation. His family gave this party. This was his childhood home. But he was alone. Why? Because he liked it that way, he thought. He'd always wanted it that way. However, it didn't seem true anymore. He ached to have a beautiful woman in his arms, inhale her sweetness and move slowly to the music with her.

He turned, trying to think of something to do to stop this introspection, and couldn't believe his eyes. He blinked. There, across the dance floor, in the wide archway, stood Faith Arden.

Faith, as delicate-looking as he remembered in slim black pants, a clingy white silk shirt and her halo of dark curls, hadn't left Wolf Lake. A throng of people shuffled between them, and he was too far away to see her eyes, but he remembered their deep blue color.

She stood out, maybe only to him, but with everyone around her laughing, talking and singing, she looked like an island of sadness in the midst of it all. She'd either lied to him about leaving, or something had made her stay in Wolf Lake. He didn't want to think she'd lied to get rid of him.

He kept sight of her as he wended his way through the milling crowd, past the dancers, then he saw her close her eyes for a moment, turn and look around as if she was searching for an escape. She found it. The doors to the west end of the barn were right behind her and she slid one back a bit. When he was within ten feet of her, she disappeared through the narrow opening.

He kept going. He eased the doors open and left the glitter and music for the more subdued light and sounds of the sprawling wing. He stopped just inside. Faith was nowhere in sight and for one crazy moment he thought he'd conjured up her image out of nothing. A soft sigh came out of the blue and he turned to glance down one aisle of stalls.

Faith was very real, with her head bowed, her hands gripping the top railing. The sight caught him off guard. The rise and fall of her slender shoulders, her pale neck and white knuckles from holding on so tightly.

He almost turned and left, embarrassed to be there, but he couldn't go. Something was wrong. He couldn't just leave.

Adam cleared his throat, and at the sound, Faith straightened and faced him, the surprise in her blue eyes intense. Right then, he knew as clearly as he knew the sun would rise in the east tomorrow that she was in trouble and, just as clearly, that he wanted to help her. Her expression shifted from shock to uncertainty and caution. There was no trace of a smile touching her full lips.

He tried to smile, while admitting to himself that, despite being off work and out of uniform, he was still a cop. He went closer, and he caught a hint of her delicate perfume.

"I'm sorry. I didn't mean to startle you," he said.

"I didn't expect anyone to be back here."

He took a step toward her. "I didn't expect you to still be in Wolf Lake, much less at this party. I thought you were long gone."

"I was supposed to be," she said a bit breathlessly. Her drink sat on the top of the wooden stall. "Things changed, but I'll be leaving soon."

Before he could respond, the sliding door

was pulled aside and Adam twisted around to see a security guard poking his head into the barn. “Oh,” he said, his eyes flicking over the two of them. “So sorry. Just worried kids might have been in here getting up to no good.”

“It’s fine,” Adam told him.

“Yes, sir,” the man said and he quietly closed the door.

Adam turned to Faith and saw the worry on her face. The guard scared her? No, just took her by surprise the way he had earlier. “So you’re extending your vacation in Wolf Lake?” Adam cringed at his inane question.

She nibbled on her lip. “Yes, I guess so,” she said and darted a furtive look at the doors. “But I’m leaving tomorrow, probably.”

She was edgy for sure. He dealt with the darker side of humanity on a day-to-day basis and knew how little goodness there could be sometimes. Maybe she was running away from someone or worried about someone finding her. Or maybe she just didn’t like him. That almost made him laugh. That would be a real shame, since he was finding himself attracted to her more and more.

"So do you need that tour guide if you're hanging around for a bit?"

She shrugged. "No, thanks. I'm fine. As I said, I'm leaving tomorrow."

"I meant what I said to you the last time we spoke."

Her eyes widened slightly. "I told you, I don't need a guide."

"No, not that. I mean, if you need someone to talk to, I'll listen."

That made her narrow her eyes and squeeze her hands together. "Oh."

He wished that she would trust him. And tell him what was going on, and if he could help, he would. If he couldn't, that would be that. But he knew that wish wasn't going to come true. Not when she kept taking quick looks at the exit doors as if measuring how long it would take her to run to them and away from him.

He drew her attention by saying, "Okay, I'll let that go. But this is a party. A party meant for fun, especially since it's almost Christmas. So why don't we have fun?"

"Excuse me?"

"Do you know how to dance?" he asked, holding her gaze.

"Well, sure, some," she stammered.

Adam hoped that his fantasy of dancing with a beautiful woman tonight might just turn into reality if he played this right. He held out a hand to her. "Dance?" he asked, giving her his best smile. He couldn't breathe for waiting for her answer.

FAITH STARED AT ADAM, angry that for one second that the thought of dancing with him could be incredibly appealing. Then she came to her senses. She should be walking away, not becoming closer. She'd gone into the stalls to be alone, to stop a wave of self-pity that had come when she'd looked at the happiness around her.

She should just get out of the vicinity of this man. But his dark gaze held hers, and her thought process was jumbled. His eyes showed true kindness, and he was so handsome. She was trying to figure out what to do next. How she could get out of there without him following her. How she could get to Mallory's truck to sit and wait for her friend so they could go back to the inn.

But her thoughts were confused, except for one clear fact. With his black hair combed straight back from his angular face and those midnight-dark eyes meeting hers, this man was dangerous to her. She realized he'd said something else, and she didn't have a clue what it had been. "Excuse me?"

He narrowed his eyes on her. "I didn't ask you to jump off a bridge, just to dance with me. You look horrified by the prospect of a simple dance."

She was upset that she wanted to dance with him, to have him hold her and move with her. "I was just trying to think, that's all," she said. It was the best answer she could come up with right then.

He stood silently, watching her. Finally, he said, "So?"

"So what?"

He flashed that dimpled smile, and the needle on her danger meter went crazy. "The dance? Could you manage to endure it?"

She started to say she wasn't feeling well, that she had to go. She would have done that and gotten away if the doors hadn't parted again with a low whooshing sound. The action was followed by music spilling into the space, the lights and noise of the party flashing everywhere in the dimly lit barn. One look at the man who had come in froze Faith to the spot.

Could things get any worse? Adam was far too close to her, and unless she was hallucinating, the policeman who had stopped her for speeding on the road to Wolf Lake was now blocking her escape. Instead of his jacket and uniform, the policeman was in a red-and-green plaid shirt with a bolo tie and jeans. For a moment, she prayed she was seeing things, but when he spoke, he shattered any particle of hope that maybe she'd been mistaken.

"Well, hello," he said. "You got here safely, I see."

He didn't give her a chance to respond, but she doubted she could have anyway. He turned to Adam. "I was starting to think you'd skipped out on the party, and then Louie told me he saw you in here." He glanced at Faith. "Although, he didn't mention you weren't alone."

She felt the air by her move as Adam came closer. "John, this is Faith. You've already met her. She's visiting around here."

The man's warm smile never faltered. "Of

course I remember her," he said. "Welcome to Wolf Lake. I hope you enjoy your stay."

"Thank you," she said.

The cop looked relaxed, as if he was there for a good time and nothing else. But she wasn't relaxing, she couldn't relax, not with Adam so near that she could literally feel his body heat. John motioned toward Adam without looking away from Faith. "Has he taken you out to see our lake yet?"

"Oh, no," she said. "I'm leaving tomorrow. I'll miss the lake, I guess."

"Too bad," he said with a teasing gleam in his eyes that she didn't quite understand. "But have fun tonight, and have a very Merry Christmas."

"Thanks," she said. The officer headed back into the main part of the barn.

She stood very still while watching him go, then Adam's breath touched her cheek as he spoke close to her ear. "Have you reconsidered that dance?"

She closed her eyes, shutting out the image of John, the lawman. Dance? She opened her eyes and the security guard was there, crossing in front of the still-open doors. He waved at Adam and her, then kept going, but not before he eyed Faith longer than she thought was a casual gesture.

Maybe if she went with Adam to the dance floor and had one dance with him they'd all think she belonged here, and then she could slip away without drawing any more attention to herself. "Sounds good," she replied, "but just one dance."

"Great," he said and led her to the dance floor, then she turned slightly and looked up into his eyes. The darkness in them seemed penetrating, as if the man could see past her feeble facade and was close to seeing the real her. Right then, she knew her mistakes were piling up. Her judgment was so flawed when Adam was around.

She was ready to get the dance over with, when he touched her arm. Even through the silk, she felt his heat, the tips of his fingers barely there, yet the world seemed centered on their connection.

"I was wondering something." Adam raised his voice to be heard over the party noise.

She steeled herself. "What?"

"Where are you staying?"

She hedged and thought she did a good job. "In the area, with a friend."

He was asking questions that should be easy to evade, and she hoped they stayed that way. "You're here with that friend?"

She nodded and wished this to be over.

"Who's your friend you're staying with? I know just about everyone in town."

As the one song finished, the first strains of "Have Yourself a Merry Little Christmas" came from the band. She didn't doubt he knew everyone, and everyone knew him. "Someone I met."

Her words sounded abrupt, and when she heard his next question, she knew she'd have to do better.

"Just wondering if the friend is male or female."

She stood there feeling exposed and uncomfortable. "What difference does that make?"

"Well, if I have to tell you that, I must be losing my touch," he murmured as he reached for her. Her breath caught when he laced his strong fingers with hers. The feeling of his other hand slipping around her back, then easing her closer to him, didn't help. He was tall enough that when they started moving, it would have been so very natural for her to lay her head on his chest. The temptation was there, but she didn't give in.

The music was all around them. The soft decorative lights, the joy of the guests, too. Her eyes stung, and she let her forehead touch Adam's chest where his jacket parted. The smoothness of his shirt was against her skin, and she hid any expression from his prying eyes. She admitted she felt an illogical sense of safety in his arms, with the beat of his heart sure and steady in her ear. She wanted nothing more than to just stay there, to let him hold her. But sanity was pushing at her and stopped the free fall into some fantasy. She had no right to it.

She moved slowly, making herself shift back a bit, then look up at dark eyes studying her, that smile shadowing his lips. How she wished this was just a party, a casual meeting between a man and a woman, but none of that was true. She stopped moving, slipped her hand carefully out of his, and as his hand left her waist, she stopped dancing. "I have to go," she said, but Adam raised his voice loud enough to be heard over the music.

"Faith?"

She made herself turn, hoping she could form a smile on her lips. He hesitated, then said simply, "Merry Christmas, Faith."

She nodded, her throat too tight for words. She kept going, afraid Adam was right behind her. She didn't stop until she stepped out into the chilly night and knew she was alone.

She put Adam and the dance behind her. It was over and done. It was a memory, nothing more. And she'd make very sure she didn't fall into a situation like this again. A woman passed her, smiled and wished her a very Merry Christmas. Faith smiled, not sure if the expression was more of a grimace than a smile, but the lady seemed okay with it.

She glanced into the huge barn and heard "I'll Be Home for Christmas" start. She was going to call her father as soon as she got back to the inn.

CHAPTER SIX

ADAM HAD WANTED to ask Faith so much more, to find a way to get beyond her vague responses to his questions. But he'd stopped himself, remembering how she'd paled when she'd seen John again. She had obviously remembered him from the traffic stop, and at best, she'd seemed uneasy, at worst, she'd seemed afraid. So Adam had kept his mouth shut.

He had gotten to dance with a beautiful woman. He'd inhaled her scent, felt her softly against him, fought an urge to kiss the top of her head, and he'd just let himself get lost in the moment.

But that moment had been over far too soon.

The man in him was disappointed, very disappointed that he hadn't been able to have more time with Faith. The cop in him was frustrated, wanting to get answers, to find out what she was doing, why and what was driving her. The man wanted to make sure that she didn't have to run from anyone, least of all him, and to protect her from anyone out to do her harm.

He had seen her briefly by the buffet, then lost sight of her as she neared Santa. Presents had been given out and children and parents alike were in a frenzy of opening their gifts.

He tried to spot her again, unaware he still stood on the dance floor. A hand came down heavily on his shoulder. He turned to face his father, who was the last person he wanted to see right then.

"You're blocking the dancers," Herbert Carson said in his deep voice as he motioned Adam toward the sidelines with a tilt of his head. "Let's let the people enjoy themselves."

Adam moved away with his father following. Although he and his father were the same height, Adam echoed his mother's heritage and little of his father's Irish American roots.

His father looked awkward and Adam knew he was losing patience with the drinks being offered at the party—straight punch and an array of sodas and bottled waters. Nothing stronger. This party had never been his idea, but his mother's. It was all for her, and his dad endured it for her sake. Endured because being a recovering alcoholic had taken its toll on his dad, and Adam appreciated how he'd stuck to his guns about never drinking again. But it wore him thin at times like this. "How's it going, son?" he asked.

"How's it going for you?" he responded, a question for a question.

The man shrugged, tugging at the slight tightness of his shirt where it buttoned at his stomach. "I put in my time, so I'm about to cut out of here." He glanced at his watch. "Over two hours." He chuckled roughly. "Longer than last time."

"I know Mom appreciates it," Adam said. He knew where his dad would go. Back to the house, into the study and on the phone to his sponsor to talk himself though the urge for alcohol.

"Yeah, well, I appreciate her and all she does," his father said with heartfelt emotion. "She deserves sainthood after everything I've put her through."

Adam recoiled from the memories of the

past, of the pain and hurt. That was gone, over with, and despite what had happened, he had his dad back. That was what counted.

"A real saint putting up with us three boys," Adam agreed.

"That she is," his father murmured. "And speaking of my sons, I haven't found Jack yet."

Adam hedged. He wanted to tell his mother first about Jack leaving. "I haven't, either," he said.

His dad patted Adam's shoulder and said, "Good to see you," then headed toward the most direct route to the house.

Adam exhaled and looked over to where he'd seen Faith last. Folks were cleaning up gift paper that seemed to be everywhere, and a bunch of kids were playing with their toys, but Faith wasn't anywhere to be seen.

He grabbed a high stool by the drinks area and spun the swivel seat to face the crowds. He couldn't spot any woman with a halo of curls and amazing blue eyes filled with uncertainty, wariness and maybe a touch of fear. Faith was gone. He checked his watch, saw it was two hours to midnight, but he knew that even when the clock struck twelve, he wouldn't find a glass slipper.

He spotted John dancing with his wife, Hannah. John caught Adam's eye over his wife's head and grimaced, as if to say, *Get me out of this,* but Adam only smiled back at him. Moses was on the farther side of the dance floor with Mallory Sanchez, and the man's expression was the direct opposite of John's. Moses was listening intently to what Mallory was saying to him, smiling at her as they moved together. It was obvious that there was no way the man wanted that dance to end.

The couple had a history of sorts, he remembered. Moses had been interested in Mallory years ago in high school, but before anything could solidify between them, Mallory had met Henry Sanchez and, as they say, the rest was history. They'd married right after graduation, and Moses had claimed he'd moved on, although he'd never married or seriously been involved with anyone for very long. Now he looked like a lovesick teenager. Maybe the time was right for Mallory to move on, and Moses was there waiting for her.

He scanned the crowd and saw his mother talking to his father before reaching up to hug him tightly. Lark Carson was dressed in her traditional costume, a very intricately fashioned elf getup that brought a smile to most faces, especially to his father's. The still-pretty dark-haired woman who barely topped five feet was still the love of his dad's life, and no matter what had gone on between them, that had never changed.

His mother was a fighter, not a quitter. He'd often wondered if that determination was a good thing or a bad thing, and pretty much settled on good for now as she stood on tiptoes to kiss his dad before he turned and left the party.

Adam made his way across the room to his mother, who spotted him as if she was expecting him right then. She smiled brightly at her son, and he hated what was coming. They hugged, then Adam pulled back to try to figure out how to tell her about Jack. He didn't have to. Before he could speak, his mother looked into his eyes and the smile drifted away.

"Jack's not coming, is he?"

The boys had often wondered if their

mother was a seer, or what his grandfather described as someone who knew things before they could be spoken of or before they could materialize. Lark said she knew because she was a mother, nothing more and nothing less. Maybe she was just that tuned into her family.

"No, he's not, Mom," he admitted to her.

"I knew he wouldn't. I've called the office for the past few days and Maureen keeps saying he's busy taking care of a client."

Jack had obviously had his assistant cover for him, which she did when it was a client, but never with the family. "She's mistaken," he said, not wanting to say she'd lied to his mother. "He actually flew out to be with Robert and his family. I'm not sure when he'll be back."

She surprised him when a second of shock turned to a soft smile. "Sweetheart, don't look so worried. This is a good thing for him. Even if he can't be here for Christmas, I think he needs this."

Adam was grateful she understood. He gave her another hug and heard her say, "Everything is fine. Although, I do wish he'd told me about going. I have some presents for Trey that he could have taken with him, instead of me having to mail them. But now that he's there, I'm happy about it. Robyn's twin might be the one to help him where we can't."

"I thought you'd be upset that Jack wouldn't be here. I know how badly you felt that Gage couldn't get back."

"I miss both my boys, but everything's okay." She touched his cheek. "Besides, you're here. That makes me very happy." She motioned to the riotous happiness all around them. "And all of this makes me very happy, too."

He followed the arc of her hand and found himself still looking for Faith. His mother startled him by asking, "Are you looking for the woman you were dancing with?"

He darted a look at her. He didn't even ask how she knew about Faith when she'd been so involved in the party. "I wondered if she—"

"She's gone," she said, "I saw her leave about ten minutes ago while you were talking to your father."

"Who did she leave with?"

"No one. She was alone, but seemed in

a hurry." She shook her head. "I felt badly that she didn't seem as if she'd been enjoying herself, even after she'd danced with the best-looking man in the room." She smiled at him. "What's that all about?"

Adam looked out across the huge space. "I don't know," he admitted. "But I wish I did."

FAITH HAD FOUND Mallory coming off the dance floor with a medium-built man with buzzed dark hair, sharp features and a height that perfectly matched Mallory's. She was smiling, a bit flushed and spoke quickly. "Faith, this is Dr. Moses Blackstar."

"Nice to meet you," she said, and seeing Mallory with such a wide smile made Faith feel foolish that she'd ever thought of not coming to the party with her. But now she was going to make her escape before anything else happened. "I'm really tired and wondered if you were ready to go." She saw Mallory glance at the doctor, who moved his head in an almost-imperceptible nod.

Mallory fished in her pocket and brought out the keys to her truck. "I'm going to stay a bit longer. Why don't you go ahead and take the truck back to the inn? It's a five-speed and a bit quirky, but it will get you there okay."

Faith thanked Mallory, then hurried to the truck. The engine bucked and sputtered at first, then settled down. She managed to reach the inn without any problems beyond the bad suspension.

She pulled up front near the stone fence and saw a motorcycle sitting where her car had been parked that first day at the inn. The bike was partially hidden under a protective tarp. There was a bit of snow on top, but she could still see the bike cover was decorated with a soaring eagle in red, white and blue. Where the tarp didn't cover the bike completely, she could make out part of a brilliant red, white and blue flame.

She went inside, expecting to see Mallory's niece, who had offered to keep an eye on the inn while Mallory was out. The young girl had arrived in an old VW Beetle done in gray primer and with an engine that sputtered. Mallory had introduced her to Faith just as she arrived. "My niece, Wallace, but we call her Wally."

The girl had looked about sixteen, her dark hair in braids, and she wore a T-shirt that proclaimed, *Hey, I might look lazy, but on a cellular level, I'm a whirlwind of activity.* "My Dad thought Wallace was a strong name, the name that some woman who married a king or something had, and it was better than what my mother wanted to call me, which was Seraphim." She'd rolled her eyes expressively. "An angel of all things." The girl, who hadn't seemed to care about missing the party because "Aunt Mallory is paying me a bundle to do this," had added with a sly grin, "I'm no angel."

But no one came out of the back now. Instead, there was movement in the sitting area and Faith turned to see Willie G. getting out of one of the chairs, stretching his arms as he yawned. "Well, well, well," he murmured, coming slowly over to her. His red, white and blue headband was askew, and his jeans and T-shirt were rumpled. "So how do you like this little town?"

She knew he was Mallory's uncle, but it was still a bit surprising to see him there. "Fine," she said. "What happened to Wally?"

"I got a call to come take over because she suddenly had to go to the party. Seems some boy named Lance would be there after all, and she wanted to 'accidentally' run into him." He looked past her. "From what Wally told me, you drove out with Mallory, but now I'm thinking you came home without her."

"She wanted to stay longer," Faith said.

"Really?" He seemed taken back. "And why would that be? Last I heard, she wasn't even sure about going, much less sticking around to all hours."

"She was enjoying the dance," she said and moved toward the stairs.

"She was dancing?" He didn't follow her, but called after her, "Who with?"

"A doctor, Moses something," she said over her shoulder.

"Moses Blackstar?"

"I think so."

"Wow," he said with feeling.

She stopped and turned with one hand on the newel post. Willie G. was grinning. "That's good?"

"Very good."

"He said he'd bring her home."

"Even better," the older man said, then cocked his head in her direction. "How about you? Did you have a good time?"

"It was nice," she answered.

"And?"

"Lots of people."

"And?"

"And lots of food and noise and music and Christmas stuff."

"What about—"

Faith cut him off. "I'm sorry, but I'm very tired."

"Sure, of course," he said. "I remember you wanted a place to rest and have some downtime." But that didn't mean that he wouldn't ask her one more question. "So did you dance, too?"

Faith started up the stairs as she said, "Once," and kept going.

"Who with?" he asked before she could get to the top level.

"Just a man." She took the last step and turned toward her room. The man's laughter could still be heard, and she almost smiled, too. Calling Adam "just a man" seemed too easy. Without even knowing much about him, she could guess that there was very little about Adam that was simple. Her reactions to him certainly weren't anywhere near simple.

Alone in her room, Faith pushed the images of the party, her time talking with Adam at the stall and the single dance with him out of her mind to try to read more of the files off the thumb drive. She opened the next one, jotted down the date it was created in her notebook and started to read. She forced herself to focus on the words and figures. An hour later, she was nearing the end of the first file.

She was ready to stop and crawl into bed to sleep. But on the second-last page, something caught her attention about Kenner Associates. She saw a contact name and number that leaped out at her from the screen. A. Z. Mason with an international phone number that had a prefix for the Cayman Islands, often a financial safe house for questionable dealings.

Her heart sank as she flipped to the last page, saw a company called Kleiner Associates with A. Z. Mason listed and the same phone number given. She found two more subdivisions of Kenner Associates, and A. Z. Mason was attached to both of them. It hit her like a thunderbolt. Mason was the key to the sting, and her dad had dealt with him directly.

They'd collaborated on a string of proxies.

It meant a way to launder more money. Tax evasion. So, finally, the truth. Or was she overreacting? The name of another related company scrolled into view on the screen, associated with A.Z Mason and her father, and she knew that she wasn't overreacting. Not at all.

Her troubles were certainly not far behind her, she thought as she stared at the screen. They were everywhere she looked. She quickly jumped up, almost knocking over the chair.

She raced to the toilet, feeling nauseous, but nothing happened. She finally sank back onto her heels and shook her head. This couldn't be a coincidence, her hearing that particular name, the company Lenz had threatened her father with, finding it in the files, and attached to a man laced through the whole sting. She wished it were otherwise. But that was silly. Facts were facts and she knew what she'd heard her father say, that he'd take care of it with Mason. He'd agreed and done it.

She slowly got to her feet, walking back into the bedroom. She snuggled under the comforter, and stared at the shadowy ceiling.

She hadn't been sure what she'd been looking for in the files, beyond anything the prosecutor might plan on using in the case against her father. She'd kind of hoped she'd know what was important when she saw it. She knew that anything to do with Kenner hadn't been aboveboard. And she knew her father had finalized whatever the agreement had been. She'd heard him promise to do just that.

The files for Kenner all looked like routine work, investment trackers, plus and minus values and projected profits, long-term goals. It seemed normal, even that three subaccounts had been opened. But the argument in her father's office hadn't been about any normal dealings. If she'd been subpoenaed, it would have been all over for her father.

She left the bed and went to get her purse. She found her cell phone and sank back on the comforter with it. She wanted to call her dad. She wanted to hear his voice, and she wanted him to convince her that she was wrong. More delusions, she thought, but finally rang her father's private number. On the third ring, he answered.

"Yes?" Raymond Sizemore asked hesitantly.

"Dad." She barely got out the word before the tears came.

"Angel? Is that you?"

Faith swiped at her eyes, forced a breath into her tight lungs and said, "I just wanted you to know I'm okay. I'm okay." And she hung up.

She had no idea if his phone line was tapped, although she thought it was a real possibility. Maybe she'd just done one more stupid, impulsive thing, but she'd had to. Hugging herself, she rocked back and forth until she got her emotions under control.

Eventually, she got undressed, climbed back into bed and switched off the light. *If you need to talk to anyone, I'm a good listener,* Adam had said, and how she wished she could talk to him, to tell him the truth, to ask for his advice.

She rolled onto her side, her foolishness weighing on her heavily. Her mind raced and her heart ached. Loneliness only made it worse.

Then logic overtook her emotions, and she realized that her decision to run to prevent being subpoenaed by the grand jury had just been validated by what she'd found. Hiding had been the best thing she could do to protect her father. And she hated it.

She glanced at the bedside clock, and it showed midnight. The door downstairs chimed, and muted voices could be heard, then the door chimed again followed moments later by an engine roaring to life out front. Willie G. was on his bike and leaving.

She shifted to her other side, tried to relax, then finally felt the first tendrils of sleep. She heard the strains of "Have Yourself a Merry Little Christmas" and felt Adam's arms around her.

She should have made herself wake up, but she let that go. She was suddenly too tired to fight anything, and she embraced a world that didn't have troubles. It had warmth and strength, and Adam. Her hand in his. His smile, the dimple and his "Merry Christmas, Faith." His voice was the last thing she remembered before she finally sank into a deep sleep.

THE NEXT THREE DAYS were made up of gray skies, thin snow on the ground, seeing old friends, and finally Adam gave in to a driving need to see if Faith was still in town. He didn't want to think that she had left Wolf Lake by now, but the fact was, she could be his past and not part of his present. She'd said something about leaving two days ago, but he didn't think that was a firm plan. He hoped it wasn't. He'd work on that premise and go from there.

By the time he dressed in jeans and a cabled sweater, he was at his computer typing in a single name on the search line, just as he'd done for the past two days. Faith Arden. The hits were many, but still none matched what he was looking for. After fifteen minutes of clicking on links and putting in variations on the name, including *Illinois, criminal record* and anything else he could think of without finding a thing, he gave up.

There had to be a Faith Arden out there from Illinois with something going on in her life that had made her leave the area. He grabbed his denim jacket and avoided both parents by not even going into the main house for breakfast. Soon, he was in his truck driving off, with a loose plan of action that he'd been mulling over since the dance. It was weak, and any chance of success would rest on whether her "friend" was a local or traveling with her. If the friend was not local, then she had to be at a motel or such in the area. If the friend was local, it would get more complicated, but doable if he got going on it.

Once he arrived in town, discovering how busy it was getting so close to Christmas, he bypassed the influx of sightseers and skiers who'd stopped for food or shopping before moving on to the higher ski areas beyond Wolf Lake.

He parked the truck on a side street away from the main section of town and called the three motels in the area. He described Faith and her car, but no one knew anything about her. He tried Mallory Sanchez at the inn, but the call went to voice mail. He hung up, then contacted the local rental company and asked about any recent short-term rentals. No Faith on any rental papers, no one from Illinois, and he realized any rental could be under the friend's name. That was a problem.

He was about ready to start driving around, then maybe head over to Mallory's Inn, when he spotted a petite woman with dark curls, bundled up in a flame-red coat and walking in the opposite direction. He was out of the truck in a second, hurrying after her. He gained on her and actually got within ten feet of her before stopping dead in his tracks.

A man in a wool cap and a brilliant orange down vest with denims and heavy boots came toward her. She practically jumped into his arms. Adam was stunned at the weight of disappointment that came down on him. Someone bumped him from the back, apologized, then hurried past, but he barely noticed. The man drew back, slipped his arm around the woman, and they kept walking, holding on to each other as they went.

He'd thought Faith was running from a man or a situation with a man, but she wasn't running from this guy, whoever he was. Maybe she'd been speeding to get to Wolf Lake to be with this man, the supposed friend she was with. The guy leaned down to say something close to her ear. Whatever he'd said, it stopped her and she turned to him. A profile with a sharp nose and strong chin were silhouetted in the grayish light of day; the features weren't even close to Faith's.

Adam closed his eyes to absorb the relief he felt that the woman wasn't Faith and his frustration that he hadn't found her. The strength of those emotions made little sense, especially when they concerned a woman he had seen three times and danced with once.

He turned to head back to the truck, admitting that he was on some crazy compulsive streak. Even when he was on the job, logic controlled him. And this wasn't logical at all. Faith was a stranger. Faith had a life somewhere with someone. But not here and not with him. It was that simple. And she certainly wasn't someone who made the news. He would give up his futile attempts using the internet and coming up empty.

He climbed into the truck, started it, then swung out onto the street and decided to head to the police station to find John. If anyone could be logical about this, John could be. He needed to talk to his friend, if for no other reason than to have him remind him of how stupid he was being.

His progress was slow, hampered by the people crisscrossing the streets and cars inching along so that folks could scan the brightly decorated shop windows. He had sat on stakeouts for hours on end, with patience that he had mastered years ago, but not being able to figure out if Faith was still in town was getting to him.

He ran a hand over his face, exhaled, then looked from side to side on the street and that was when he saw "Faith" again.

The woman who looked like Faith was small and quick, with black curls, dressed in jeans, chunky boots and a heavy red sweater that seemed to engulf her. He didn't look for a parking spot to stop and go after her. Instead, he watched her go, her head down, her chin nestled in the thick yarn of the sweater as she veered to her right, then took the steps up and into the general store. He wasn't aware he'd stopped the truck in the middle of the street until a horn blared behind him. He wasn't going on another wild-goose chase.

He quickly pulled ahead and found himself outside Mallory's Inn. He almost drove on, but then changed his mind. He got out, jogged to the door and went inside. A chime sounded as he looked around the deserted reception area. "Mallory," he called, going to the desk, but no one answered.

He tried again. "Mallory?"

"Excuse me?" Someone spoke from behind him, and he turned to see a couple sitting in the lounge area by the fireplace. The man was nursing a steaming mug, and the woman with him was mirroring his actions. They both looked expectant.

"Excuse me," Adam said. "I'm looking for the owner."

"She's gone for a bit. Said she'd be back as soon as she could," the man said.

Adam thought it was worth a try to ask, "Do you know how many guests are staying here?"

"We're not sure," he said, glancing around. "We only checked in a few hours ago, a room at the back down here on the first floor. To be honest, we haven't seen or heard anyone."

Adam spotted the ledger on the desk, crossed to it and was about to reach for it when his phone rang. He checked the caller ID. Jack. He thanked the couple and headed out as he hit the talk button on the phone. "Jack?"

"It's me," his older brother said over the line.

Adam hopped into the truck and waited, then finally spoke when Jack didn't. "How are things up north?"

There was an intake of breath, then Jack said, "Just checking in."

Adam glanced behind him, switched on the ignition and backed out into the street. "What is it?"

"I said, I'm—"

"You called to tell me something. What is it?"

"I'm staying here until after the New Year."

"Things are going okay?"

"Yes, they are. Trey's a great kid, and…" His voice trailed off and then he tried again. "He looks a lot like his dad." It meant he looked a lot like Robyn, too. "He's a good kid."

Adam smiled. "I bet he is. Tell Robert to bring him out to see Mom and Dad as soon as he's able to."

"Will do," Jack said, then added, "Merry Christmas." He hung up.

Adam exhaled. Jack was okay. He was working things out. And he'd be back sooner or later. He just needed time. Meanwhile, here he was running around like a chicken with his head cut off looking for a woman who was probably hundreds of miles away from Wolf Lake.

He was a cop who had tracked down a number of people, and yet now he'd lost a woman who seemed to be able to flit in and out of his life at will. He couldn't find one pretty, dark-haired woman in a town a fraction of the size of Dallas.

He drove away from the inn, spotted the police station and pulled into the parking lot. It couldn't hurt to at least talk to John. If nothing else, he could complain to his friend about the way life worked sometimes. He got out and to the door of the flat-roofed, sprawling building with a handful of cruisers out front. He was way out of his jurisdiction, but at this point he was beyond caring.

Jack should be his focus, not a woman who didn't seem to want him anywhere near her. As he stepped inside, he almost ran into John. They avoided a collision, made small talk, and by the time they were in John's office, Adam had decided not to discuss Faith or admit to the obsession he had. That was gone. She was gone. They talked about John's family, the holidays and Jack's phone call.

When Adam left a half hour later, he felt

settled and focused. Until he got back in the truck. It wasn't obsessive to want some information about Faith. It was what he did. And he was like his mother and was not a quitter. He turned the motor on, got the heater blowing warm air, then sat back and took out his cell phone. He put in a call to his partner in Dallas, and when Connors picked up, he said, "Hey, it's Adam and I need you to do me a favor."

CHAPTER SEVEN

FAITH STOOD, EXAMINING the sundries at the general store. She had a jumble of thoughts going through her mind, things that confused her and things that made her heart ache. It had been hours since she'd gotten up and started hunting through the files. But now her stomach grumbled.

It was midmorning and she'd finished the last of her supplies—the granola bars, crackers and candy that she kept in her room along with packets of instant coffee. The coffee she brewed on a hot plate on her dresser.

As soon as she'd ducked inside the general store, she spotted the old man who seemed to own the place. Oscar Ortega, a balding man in his early seventies, was intently polishing a display of snow globes on a glass case near the window. He looked up as soon as the door opened.

"Well, good morning, missy. It's a great day," he said, the same greeting he'd used every time she'd visited.

"Good morning," Faith had replied and picked up an empty shopping basket, walking back to the grocery area.

"Got some of that fancy creamer in, if you want to try some," he called after her.

"Thanks," she said and ducked into the dry-goods aisle, where she reached for the packets of instant coffee. After debating with herself whether to buy both cookies and chips, she decided she had all that she needed and went to pay. As she passed the newspaper stand, she glanced at the news and stopped abruptly.

A copy of a national newspaper had slipped off the stack, and its sections had separated and splayed on the floor. The headline of the business section reflected her worst nightmare. She crouched, pulling that section free with a shaky hand, then stood and stared at six photographs lined up neatly, head and shoulder shots.

Raymond Sizemore was dead center, his partners on either side and the top financial officers from the company filling in the last squares. Above the pictures were the words *Grand Jury Indictments?* and below, a blurb about testimony starting today in the case against… Faith didn't know if she should drop the paper and run, or stand there and cry.

Aware that Oscar was watching her from the cash register, she reached down for the rest of the newspaper sections and pushed the financial one out of sight between them. She put the paper on the counter and almost forgot the basket sitting on the floor by her feet. She didn't even remember putting it down. Quickly, she grabbed it, pushed the newspaper on top of the food and drinks, then looked at Oscar.

"Hungry, huh?" he said conversationally as he scanned the contents of her basket.

"A bit," she murmured. "What do I owe you?"

He gave her a total and she paid cash. Then she reached for the two bags he'd stacked her things in, thanked him and headed for the door.

"Oh, missy," Oscar called after her.

She turned. "Yes?"

He was smiling at her and holding out

something for her. "Here, take these. Try them, and when you come back in, you might want a few to make that instant coffee drinkable."

Reluctantly, she hurried over to him and he dropped the small creamers in the nearest bag she was holding.

At the inn, she felt sick as she dumped her bags on the bed in her room and dug out the newspaper. Spreading the financial section on the still-unmade bed, she read quickly about the possible indictment, other grand-jury witnesses that she had never heard of and the fact that the prosecutor was saying the process could be lengthy.

She followed the story to an inside page and breathed a huge sigh of relief when she found no photos attached to that section. There was also no mention of her at all. Was that planned, or was that because she had been dropped from the possible-witnesses list?

She closed the paper, folded it several times and placed it in the trash can by the bed. She dropped down on the bed by the bags and reached to pick up her cell phone. She turned it on for the first time since she'd called her dad the night of the dance and put in Dent's number. The phone rang several times before going to an answering machine. She hung up.

She decided to walk over to Dent's and find out about her car. The piece in the paper had really affected her—all she could think of was getting on the move and not stopping for days. Her forced stay in Wolf Lake had not done her any favors. She grabbed her jacket and slipped it on.

She was getting tangled up with these people, good people, kind people, from Mallory to Oscar to Willie G. to Adam. But they were finding out too much about her, and if there had been a picture with that article… She picked up her wallet and stepped out into the hallway. She paused and listened, then looked over the banister. The people by the fire were gone, and no one was by the desk.

She hurried down, got almost to the front door when she heard, "Hey, Faith!" and turned to see Mallory coming through the swinging door.

Her friend was all smiles, just as she had been since the party. "Lovely day, isn't it?" she said, almost singing the words as she came around the desk.

Not really, Faith thought. But she wouldn't say that. She looked at Mallory, at the flush in her cheeks and the softening of her features. It wasn't hard to figure out that the doctor's regular visits to the inn ever since the dance were probably responsible for the glow. "Yes, it's nice out. Cold, but nice."

Mallory grinned and straightened the registration book. "Where you off to?"

"Dent's. To find out about my car."

"Good luck," she said, then cocked her head to one side. "I was talking to Willie G. last night, and you know what he told me?" She didn't wait for an answer, but supplied it herself. "He told me that you were dancing at the party. So tell me about it."

No, she wouldn't. "It was just a dance," Faith said, feeling tension in her neck. "One dance." Then she turned to leave.

"Wait," Mallory said, stopping Faith before she'd taken another step. "I need your advice."

More advice? Another reason she shouldn't have allowed herself to get familiar with the people here. "What about?"

"Moses. He asked me out to dinner, but

I'm not sure. I mean, I'd love to go, but I'm not sure I should."

Faith cocked her head to one side to study Mallory for a moment. "And why not? He's been around here all the time since the dance."

Mallory's cheeks reddened. "It feels odd, like, really strange. I kind of thought that I could..." She finally met Faith's gaze. "Would you go, if you were me?"

Faith was having trouble with her own life and her choices and wasn't in any position to be handing out advice to others. And if Mallory knew about the mess, she wouldn't be asking her for the time of day. "I'm not you and I've never been married or even engaged. But if you want to go, go. If you're too uncomfortable about it, suggest that you go on a double date or something. That would make it less intense, I'd think."

Mallory was silent, and then she nodded slowly. "Yes, go out with others or maybe go to some place that's crowded and not so intimate. Yes, I think that might work. It makes sense."

Faith cut in before Mallory could go on. "I need to get over to Dent's."

Mallory smiled. "Oh, of course, I'm sorry. Sure, go ahead, but don't think I'll forget that I owe you for this."

"Don't even think about it." Faith reached for the door latch but didn't make it outside.

Mallory asked, "Who did you dance with at the party?"

She thought of lying, but didn't. "Someone named Adam."

"Adam?" Mallory repeated. "Adam." She glanced at Faith, and then she looked shocked. "Not Adam Carson?"

Faith shook her head. "I don't know. He didn't say."

"Did he have that Carson look?"

"What Carson look?"

"Tall, gorgeous, dark eyes, a sort of look that could be Native or cowboy? And sexy."

That about described the Adam she knew. "I guess that's him."

"Oh, my goodness!" Mallory exclaimed. "Adam Carson. Wow!"

The knot in Faith's stomach and the tension in her neck were growing by the second. "Glad that's a good thing."

"Glad? Well, I'm sure happy for you. Adam Carson is the middle Carson boy. Never married, totally eligible and back home for the holidays. How great is that? Are you going to go out or anything?"

Horror gripped Faith. "No, no, of course not. It was one dance, and that was that." Then she lied like crazy. "No sparks, no flame, no nothing. Just a dance."

Mallory actually looked disappointed, and at any other time, Faith would have laughed at the expression on her face. But she didn't laugh as Mallory dropped a bomb on her. "Probably just as well. He's a wanderer and a cop. What a combination, huh?"

Faith stared at the woman, shocked. "A cop?"

"Yes, in Dallas. He was one here for a short time, then he left, got on somewhere else, then after a few more changes, he ended up in Dallas. The man isn't built to stay in one place too long or for making any sort of commitment, I guess." She frowned. "Sorry, it's just he's never been married, not even close from what I heard."

Faith hated the way her heart was assaulting her ribs, beating so hard she was certain Mallory could tell. "I really need to go," she said in a surprisingly even voice. "See you later." Faith pulled the door open and closed and this time didn't even feel the cold.

The walk to the garage only took fifteen minutes, and those fifteen minutes gave her time to absorb the fact that Adam was a policeman. She had been so close to…to what? She didn't even know. Adam Carson. Obviously part of the wealth she'd only glimpsed at the party. A founding family of some sort, she thought. Three sons. Adam was the second one. A sexy cop. She chuckled wryly at that. Of course he was sexy, but that didn't matter to her. What was devastating was that he was a cop.

She spied Dent working on her car and learned that he finally thought he knew what the problem was. But he'd have to redo another part of the electrical to know if he'd figured it out for sure. Give him another day or two. She didn't have a choice but to agree and head back toward the inn.

Even on her way there, amid her disappointment that she was stuck in Wolf Lake, Adam Carson surfaced in her thoughts. Avoid him. That was simple. Stay at the inn, in her room, except for food runs. That was all she could do. She got back to her room without seeing anyone. She locked the door and started to strip off her jacket and kick off her boots, and still she fought the image of Adam with his dark eyes. Cop's eyes. If he ever knew who was in his little town... She shook her head sharply, a pain radiating down into her shoulders. She rubbed the back of her neck. He'd never know. She'd be long gone soon, and she was nothing to him, nothing he'd remember.

She took a seat in the chair in front of the computer, slowly rotating her head until the pain was fading. She went online, did a search for her father's name and the company name, linking both with the words *federal investigations, grand jury* and *indictments.* She was gratified to see that the first explosion of articles and reports were from a few weeks ago. They diminished to updates until two days ago when the indictments had become more than a possibility. Nothing new from that, either.

The only pictures of her were old and almost unrecognizable to her. They featured a slim woman, dark hair worn slicked back from a face with sleek makeup. Perfectly tailored suits and heels made her look sophisticated and businesslike. She got up and went to the mirror in the bathroom. She faced the new Faith Sizemore and knew that this woman was nothing like the original.

Her face was pale, her hair a wild riot of curls, no lipstick, definite shadows at her cheeks and eyes, and shapeless clothes. Nothing like she'd been and, she knew, she'd ever be again. She just had to keep as low a profile as possible. No more making friends. No more giving anyone advice. And no more dancing with a cop.

She crossed back to the computer and switched from the internet to another file. She was searching for any more mentions of A. Z. Mason with Kenner or the related companies. This had to be her focus. Not Adam. Not the dance. Not the feeling of him when he'd held her. Not him being a police officer. Her father's problems had to have her full attention. Not someone who was nothing to her other than a man she found attractive and who, under other circumstances, she would have wanted to get to know better.

She shook her head, as if that could clear it of thoughts of Adam. She reviewed only one page before she found references to an

R. Sizemore deal authorized by Z. Mason. The man was listed as the main contact for another company with two subsidiaries. More and more things piled up against her father, and more and more she couldn't dismiss them.

She knew that none of the subsidiaries of Kenner Associates were legitimate. Running computer checks on them would be a waste of time.

The name A. Z. Mason stood out like a sore thumb, although whoever A. Z. Mason was, he or she had kept any images off the internet. It smelled fishy to her, and she had no doubt that it would smell fishy to anyone else who knew about the investment world. Obviously, her father had fallen for his line completely.

She sat back, feeling sick at the conclusions she was coming up with. However, she realized her queasiness was also due to something else. She felt terrible, lethargic and she just wanted to lie down.

When she finally did so, stretching out on the bed, she noticed her hands were trembling. Her vision began to blur, and suddenly she knew what was happening to her.

She'd had horrible migraines in college after cramming for exams, and she recognized the signs of one starting now. She had to do something to stop this before it gained any more force.

Faith got up, closed the drapes, turned off the lights and computer, and took some over-the-counter pain medicine. Breathing calmly, she hoped the migraine would just go away.

Instead, a few minutes later, the first fingers of pain started invading her head and neck, and she willed herself to relax.

She'd never expected this to happen, but it was happening, right down to the tingling in her hands and feet. She exhaled and thought of a beach, the sun and sand. Thankfully, sleep soon claimed her.

But when she awoke, the pain was enough to make her stomach sick. She pried her eyes open and saw the numbers of the digital clock formed 7:15. Either she'd slept all night and it was morning, or she'd been asleep for a couple of hours. No light showed around the crack in the drapes and there were muffled sounds below. Probably the evening.

Pain grew when she tried to move and she lay back. Despite the sleep, she felt exhausted and weak. She needed something else for the pain, something stronger. She forced herself to make the effort to sit and ease on her boots. Finally standing, she put on her jacket and left the room.

Her progress was ridiculously slow, but she made it down the stairs in one piece. With the door in sight and no one behind the desk, she started across the rug, but stopped when Mallory appeared from the sitting area.

Mallory came toward her, and her ever-present smile faded. “What’s wrong?” she asked, clearly concerned.

“A headache,” she breathed. “I need to go get something for it.”

“Just wait here. I’ve got something you can take.”

“No, please, it’s a migraine. I already took some over-the-counter pills.” She grimaced. “I’ll go down to the pharmacy and get something there.”

“Nothing they sell there is going to help. You need a doctor. The only place open is the E.R. at the hospital.”

Faith needed something that would work, and she needed it right away. She was going to have to put her fear of being discovered aside, at least temporarily. "How close is the hospital?"

"Too far to walk, but I can drive you," she said, then immediately shook her head. "Oh, shoot, I can't, not right now. I've got a late arrival, a couple from Boston who are going to be here over Christmas and New Year's. If you're okay to drive, you can take my truck."

Faith whispered, "Thank you." She was truly grateful for Mallory's friendship at that moment.

"Sure," she said, hurrying to the desk and returning with her keys. "I'll call Moses and let him know that you're coming. He's on call tonight." She passed the keys to her. "Are you sure you can drive okay?"

"I'll manage," Faith said. After getting directions to the hospital from Mallory, she stepped out onto the porch and felt the cold like a vice around her head. The pain almost exploded behind her eyes, and she wanted to run to the old truck. Knowing that wasn't wise, she went slowly and cautiously, opened the driver's door and eased in behind the wheel. When she put the key in the ignition and turned it, the old truck chugged to life, the cab shaking like a blender as the motor tried to find some rhythm.

She knew she couldn't do this, that she couldn't take the pain without being sick. Driving all the way to the hospital would be too much for her. She cut the engine and breathed a sigh of relief to have the movement stop. Taking a deep breath, she tried to visualize a place warm and soothing. But that wasn't about to happen while shivering in this freezing truck.

She got out, carefully slipping down onto the gravel walkway. A cab. She could call a cab. Or maybe Willie G. could wait at the inn for the new guests, and Mallory could give her a lift. She felt dizzy and grabbed the truck's fender to steady herself.

She heard a car coming close, then closer. Mallory's late arrivals? She barely glanced in the direction of the noise, saw a huge black truck slip into the slot beyond Mallory's pickup and turned away from it.

"Faith?"

The voice was familiar, but she didn't know who had spoken until she turned back. Adam. As he approached her, his smile grew wider.

"So it is you," he said.

She looked up at him, his image starting to blur. She really needed to get out of there. "What do you want?" The question was harsh, but she couldn't help it—she felt scared and like miserable.

"You," he murmured, but his smile started to slip as he studied her face. "Hey, are you okay?"

She felt weak and wanted to get inside. The world was blurring more, and she was starting to feel nauseous again.

Adam was not touching her, but he was so close he could have. He was right in front of her now. "What's wrong?" he asked.

"Migraine. I…I was on my way to the hospital, but…" She touched her tongue to her lips and felt the coldness of snowflakes on her face as she tried to look up at Adam. She hadn't noticed it had started to snow. "The truck… I can't… It's so rough."

He exhaled, the action sending a plume of his breath into the night sky. "Give me the key and I'll take care of it," he said, extending one hand to her and sounding like the cop that he was.

"No," she said. He was the last person she wanted helping her.

He reached for her, caught her hand and took the key from her. "Stay put," he said and he ran into the inn. He was there and back before she could figure out what to do to get away from him.

"I told Mallory that I'm taking you to the hospital." When he began to blur again in front of her eyes, she knew she couldn't fight him, and he seemed to know it. "I'd offer to let you take my truck, but you're in no condition to drive anything right now."

She wasn't in any condition to do anything, including making an escape. A person who didn't have anything to hide would agree with him and just be grateful he'd shown up. She decided to be that person. Growing pain trumped any other concerns she might have in that moment.

"Thank you," she whispered.

Adam held her arm and got her into his truck smoothly, easily lifting her into the cab. She welcomed the warmth and the soft leather seat.

Then he was leaning over her, snapping her seat-belt buckle. He moved back and shut the door. Faith let her head sag back against the headrest and felt the truck shift as Adam joined her. As soon as the truck roared to life, she could feel the heat flooding into the cab.

With the waves of warmth, she felt a certain edge leaving her pain. She closed her eyes and tried to think of anything but the painful throbbing.

She couldn't, not even the fact that she was alone with him, a cop, and they were heading off into the night together.

CHAPTER EIGHT

"HEY, THERE," ADAM SAID, and it startled Faith until she realized he was on his cell phone. "I'm heading your way with a woman who is in the middle of a really bad migraine." He listened for a minute, then said, "Oh, good, great. We'll be there in five." She felt him shift in his seat as he drove. He didn't say anything else. It was probably a tactic he used as a cop, keeping silent, hoping the criminal would say something incriminating. But she wasn't about to. She kept silent, too, and found it soothing.

As they took a sharp corner, the truck bounced over a pothole. The big vehicle lurched, throwing her forward in her seat against the restraint of the belt. The pain flared fiercely, and she must have cried out because Adam immediately covered her clenched hand on her thigh with his. The contact was strong and sure, and she didn't have the heart or desire to pull away from it.

"Sorry," he said to break the silence in the cab.

She saw lights glowing ahead and a glass-and-steel structure with *Wolf Lake Medical Center* above the doors. The building dominated that part of the town. Adam drove into the parking lot, swinging left toward a flashing red sign that advertised the emergency-room entrance.

He pulled into the spot closest to the double glass doors and was around to open her door before she had her seat belt undone. He looked up at her, then put his hands around her waist and lifted her up and out of the truck. Her feet touched the concrete drive, and Adam's touch on her steadied her even though her head was starting to swim again.

He shifted his hold, his arm slipping around her shoulders, and he gently tucked her to his side. His support got her to the now-open doors and inside a waiting area. Immediately, they were buzzed through to the examination rooms and doctors' station. "Dr. Blackstar is expecting us," Adam said.

As soon as Adam finished speaking, a

doctor was coming toward them, his white coat open to show a plaid flannel shirt underneath, and Faith remembered Dr. Blackstar from the dance when he'd been with Mallory.

A stethoscope was draped around his neck, and it swung back and forth as he rushed up to them with a wheelchair he was pushing. He nodded to Adam, then turned his full attention to Faith. "Sit, and I'll get you into a room," he said in a no-nonsense voice. He didn't give her a chance to object to being in a wheelchair, and to be honest, Faith didn't mind sitting down.

She wanted to thank Adam, but she couldn't make the words come. Unexpectedly, he reached out, touched her cheek with the tips of his fingers and said softly, "Moses is the best. He'll take good care of you."

She felt ready to cry at the contact and chalked that response up to the pain and sickness. Nothing made sense to her just then, least of all the fear she suddenly had that Adam was going to leave her there. She should be wanting him to go. And of course, he would. He'd driven here, and that was what he'd offered.

But when he glanced at the doctor and said,

"Let's go," Faith was inordinately thankful Adam wasn't deserting her just yet. Soon enough he'd be gone, but right then she wanted to have someone there. She wanted the very man she'd pledged to avoid until she could leave Wolf Lake. She knew that with him at her side she could get through this.

ADAM HADN'T BEEN about to walk away from Faith. He knew this hospital like the back of his hand from the months and months his brother Gage had been the lead contractor on the project. Adam had been around to follow its progress and see the results. Now he was leading Moses and Faith into the first free examination room. Moses got Faith to the side of the bed, then helped her up and out of the chair. He eased her onto the lowered examination table, then raised the bed, all the time speaking quickly, asking about her symptoms. She closed her eyes, her expression a grimace and her skin pale, but she quietly answered his questions.

He took her vitals and glanced at Adam. "Give us ten," he said, "and I'll be out to see you."

Adam was surprised he felt so reluctant

to leave her, but he finally did, wishing her eyes were open so he could at least smile at her before going. But that didn't happen, so he turned and headed back out to the waiting area.

He sat down and leaned back, staring unseeingly at a flickering TV right across from him.

Before finding her earlier, he'd accepted that Faith had left Wolf Lake. That she'd slipped away just as she had from the dance. It became real for him when his partner in Dallas let him know that he couldn't find a thing about a Faith Arden that matched the description provided in any databases he had access to.

Right then, it had been done, finished, and he'd moved on, but that didn't mean he hadn't looked back. Or that he'd forgotten Faith.

Then he'd talked to Jack again and was stunned to find out his older brother was considering something drastic, moving to be near Robert and his family. That had come out of left field, but he'd tried to be supportive, saying, "Do what you have to do for you, Jack," and he'd meant it. He wanted his brother to be happy again, to enjoy his life.

Two hours ago Adam had come into town for dinner with John and Hannah at their house, and all three agreed that at least Jack was moving on, not in a direction any of them had anticipated, but he was moving. That was all good. They'd reminisced and laughed, and Adam felt an easing in his soul. Jack would be okay, just not here in Wolf Lake.

Then he'd left his friends, driven down the street, taking in the signs of Christmas and the new snowfall, and done a double take. He'd slowed the truck, certain he was starting up his obsession again with any petite woman who might look like Faith Arden.

This one, however, was getting out of Mallory's old truck. An illusion, obviously, but as he got closer, he couldn't pass it off as such. There was something about her, and he found himself pulling into the parking area of the inn.

That was when he knew he wasn't hallucinating—this woman was Faith, standing very still as snow fell around her. Faith. He opened his door, almost afraid when he did that she'd disappear, but she didn't.

He'd about given up on ever seeing her

again. Hadn't even checked back with Mallory to find out about her guests. He'd let it go, and she'd been there all this time. Not only that, he was smack in the middle of Faith's life now. He ran a hand roughly over his face, then turned to the closed doors to the examination area. He couldn't believe he'd failed so miserably at finding her. Some cop, he thought with real self-anger. Too emotional, too involved to see the forest for the trees.

It was only dumb luck that had put her in front of him when he'd stopped looking. But now he knew what he was going to do. He was going to get answers.

Another twenty minutes passed and the doors slid back to reveal Moses pushing Faith in the wheelchair. They came toward Adam as he got to his feet. Faith looked pale but the lines of pain that had etched her face earlier seemed less pronounced. He wanted to touch her, to tell her she'd be okay even though he didn't know if she would be, or if he had any right to say or do any of that. Shoving his hands into his jacket pockets, he glanced at Moses.

"Well, it is a migraine and I've given her a

shot that should help rather quickly, and she has other medication that will help when the shot wears off." Moses said with emphasis, "She will be just fine."

Why was he so relieved that she'd be okay? He let that question go and met her gaze, her lids heavy and the long, dark lashes shadowing her eyes. She murmured her thanks. He wasn't sure if she meant that for him or Moses, or the whole hospital.

"Oh, no problem," Moses said. "Give that shot time to work, and take it easy for a few days. Stay inside and you'll be fine before Christmas. Just no driving for a day or two."

For some reason Faith looked as if she was about to smile at his order, then the expression was gone, as if it had never existed. "I won't," she said.

"You sure it's not anything more than a migraine?" Adam asked, keeping his eyes on Faith.

"A migraine is not anything minor, but yes, I'm sure it's a migraine, and she'll be okay. Just get her back to the inn and out of this weather."

A nurse approached them. "Come on, sweetie, and I'll take you to the billing area to get that over with," the woman said as Moses moved back to let her roll the wheelchair to a clerk at a nearby counter.

As soon as she was out of earshot, Adam asked in a lowered voice, "You're sure about this?"

"Hey, I got a license saying I can be sure about what I am sure about. So, yes, I'm sure."

He watched Faith start to sign some papers. "What did she tell you about herself?"

Moses narrowed his eyes as Adam looked at him. "You know I can't say much because of the privacy rules. I mean, she's not your family or anything, is she?"

She was something to him, but he couldn't sort that out right now. "I know, I know, I just wondered if there was anyone to notify for her." That was at the bottom of his list of things he'd like to know about her, but it was a start.

"I asked if there was anyone I could call for her, but she insisted there wasn't. I tried to get a name in case things went wrong, but she kept saying there was no one."

"Does her insurance cover this?" he asked.

The doctor exhaled with a touch of exasperation. "Adam, don't do this to me."

"Is it a secret if she has insurance or not?"

"Okay, no insurance. She's paying for it with cash."

"Why's she around here?" Adam asked, anxious for more information.

"Because she is. You know that theory about no one being able to occupy two separate spaces at one time?"

"I don't watch sci-fi movies, but thanks for letting me know about that theory," Adam muttered sarcastically.

"Hey, just because we're friends doesn't mean I'm going to violate any—"

Adam held up his hand to stop Moses. "Okay, I know. I won't ask if she talked about any problems she had that led her here."

"Thank you." Moses sighed. "You know, you're on vacation from being a cop. Why not enjoy it?"

Adam thought of something important, at least it was to him. "One last thing?"

"No, I can't tell you her blood type," Moses responded facetiously.

"All I want to know is if you noticed anything about her that bothered you."

"What do you mean?"

He glanced at Faith, who was at the cashier's desk, pulling her wallet out of her jacket pocket. He couldn't even explain his own question, so he gave up. "Never mind," he said. He'd find out on his own why she'd let him believe she was staying with a friend in town and why she was still here when she was supposedly leaving. He didn't need to pull Moses into any of this for answers about the woman.

"Okay," Moses murmured.

Adam looked right at his friend and couldn't stop himself. "If you thought she was in trouble of some sort, would you tell me?"

Moses studied him, glanced at Faith, then shook his head. "No. You're not family or even, as far as I know, a friend, so why would I? I'd most likely mention it to John before I'd tell you about it…if it were true."

Moses was a direct man, no hedging with him, and he'd given Adam a straight answer. He didn't like it, but it was what it was. "Thanks," he said.

A smile came to the doctor. "You asked."

"Yes, I did." He watched the nurse wheel Faith back over to the two of them.

The nurse handed her some folded papers that she laid on top of the wallet resting in her lap. "Take care of yourself and get better, dear," the woman said to Faith before she walked off.

Adam went around to grip the wheelchair handles as Moses asked, "Any word from Jack?"

"Seems he's thinking of moving to be closer to Robert and his family."

Moses looked surprised. "He won't. He's the one person who can never leave Wolf Lake."

That was what Adam had always thought, but he'd started to wonder if he'd missed the fact that Jack needed a change. "Maybe," he said.

Moses touched Faith on the shoulder. "If you need anything else, I'll be right here all night. Just call or come on back."

She nodded slightly as she closed her eyes. Adam looked at Moses over Faith's head. "Anything else she might need?"

"Just to take care of herself," Moses said and started for the waiting area.

Adam pushed the wheelchair over to the exit and rolled Faith out into a night of fine but persistent snow. The truck was close by, so he was able to push the wheelchair to the passenger side, then as she gripped her wallet and the papers, he helped her into the truck cab.

Once they were both settled and on their way, Faith with her eyes closed, Adam noticed she wasn't wearing any rings. It sounded as if she didn't have anyone, or at least anyone she wanted to know where she was or what had happened. A woman like this? That didn't seem possible.

He flicked his gaze over the dark curls brushing her forehead, and the long sweep of her lush lashes. There had to be someone out there waiting for her or looking for her, worrying about her.

When his phone vibrated in his pocket, he pulled over and glanced at the caller ID. Moses's private line. He frowned as all sorts of thoughts flew through his mind, starting and ending with more being wrong with Faith than Moses had thought at first.

He hit the talk button and said, "What's going on?"

"I've got a problem."

His eyes went to Faith again, and tightness in his throat grew. "What?"

"Merry Brenner just brought something to my attention." Merry was a child psychologist at The Family Center, a place connected to the hospital that offered help to Native children and other kids in the area with special needs. He'd never met Merry, but from what he'd heard about her from the folks in town, she had a real gift for working with the children. "She needs to talk to you, Adam."

"What about?"

"A problem. I tried John first, but he's already out on a call, got the deputy with him. They won't be free for a while, and I thought, since you're a cop and local, you might be able to help her out."

He never took his eyes off Faith, and he was impatient to get this call over with. "What is it?"

"Here's Merry. Let her explain."

The next thing he knew, a soft, feminine voice was on the line. "This is Merry Brenner. I am so sorry to bother you like this, but there's a boy in the pediatric ward at the hospital, one of the kids from The Family

Center, Brandon Sage. He's eight years old, and he had an accident a few hours ago. He was home alone and thought he could tag a hawk perched on the peak of their porch roof. So he climbed up, but fell off because of the snow. Thank goodness a neighbor saw it happen and brought him to the hospital."

She took a breath and continued, "I've tried and tried to contact the parents, and Brandon doesn't know where they went, just that they left him home alone. He's hurt and scared. He has high-functioning autism, and he needs the reassurance of his mother or father. Doctor Blackstar said you're good at finding people, and he said you know this town and the people around here."

He had thought that once, too. "Go on," he said.

"I'll stay right here with him for as long as it takes, but is there any way you could try to find his mother or father, or both of them, for him?"

He stared at Faith, then heard a soft sigh and knew she had fallen asleep. He was so intent on watching the easing in her face and thinking about her that he almost didn't hear

Merry's next words. "I understand if you're too busy."

"I'll do what I can, but I can't promise anything."

"Thank you, thank you," she said with feeling.

Then Moses was speaking. "The kid really will appreciate this."

"Is he Bingo Sage's boy?"

"That's him. They're living out by Willie G.'s old place now. Past it, on the north side. There's a rusted-out tractor blocking the driveway. We called only a minute ago and still no answer."

"Got any idea where to start looking?"

"Any of the bars for Bingo, and Norma just doesn't go many places, except out to the res to visit Big Mike, her uncle, but he doesn't believe in phones." Michael "Big Mike" Swayne had always been on the tribal council in one position or another, and Adam knew exactly where to find him. "Okay, I'll call you if I find either one." He hit End on the phone and looked at Faith. He had to get her back to the inn first, then he'd try to find the Sages.

Faith Arden. A woman who had no one

to care about her. As her tongue touched her lips, his mind went to dark places out of habit. Answers to questions on the job were seldom uplifting and nice. They usually confirmed the worst side of humanity. Optimism wasn't his strong suit by any stretch of the imagination and it wasn't getting any stronger.

She sighed again, shifting to cuddle into the corner made by the seat and the door. He saw her lip quiver slightly, then another sigh came. One way or the other, he'd figure out the puzzle that was Faith Arden. Meanwhile, he'd promised Merry Brenner that he'd track down the Sages. He focused on where to start his search.

Bars. He knew of several around town, most of them having been there since forever, and going from one to the other would be interminable. But he wanted to try a few before going all the way to the res, especially if it began snowing any harder. The roads to the res were tough at best.

There was a speedier solution, he thought, and he'd take it. He pulled over again and pushed a number into his cell phone. When a man's voice barked, "Yeah?" Adam grinned.

"Hey, Chief, is that you?"

"Big as life and twice as natural," Johnson Means said gruffly.

Johnson Means had been with Adam in school from the second grade on when his parents had moved off the res and into town. His grandfather, Wilson Means, had been the tribal head, and the kids had given Johnson the label Chief by default. The man did his own thing, and he was a great gossip, had something on everyone in town. "And just as ugly?" Adam countered with a smile.

"Depends who's looking and who made this phone ring," he growled.

"The one guy who understands why you've been divorced four times," Adam said.

"Well, you old dog, Adam. I heard you were in town, but since you never came by Hazel's, I figured it was a vicious rumor and you were off arresting the bad guys."

Adam smiled. "And I figured you were gone, especially since you weren't at the party. Never thought you'd be at your sister's."

"You were at the party?" The snort in the man's voice said it all. Neither one had gone to the party for years.

"Believe it or not, I was," he said, automatically glancing at Faith sleeping so close to him. "Hey, I need some help."

"Name it."

"You know Bingo Sage? He's living over by Willie G.'s old place?"

"What do you need to know about the guy?"

"His son got hurt falling off a roof, and he's nowhere to be found. Neither is the mom, Norma. I'm trying to find them for Moses and the psychologist Merry Brenner from The Family Center."

"Hold on for a sec," he said. Adam could hear muffled voices in the background. "Hazel says that she heard from Oscar at the store that Bingo's a fixture at the Green Arrow lately, that old hole-in-the-wall bar over on Second Street. And Norma's still a homebody."

"She's not home now."

"Then check with Big Mike on the res."

"Yeah, I might have to."

After agreeing to meet up with Chief soon, Adam hung up and looked over at a still-sleeping Faith. "Guess we'll get you home," he murmured and was startled when Faith whispered on a sigh, "Okay."

He'd thought she was asleep. "You all right?" he asked.

"Good, nice," she said, and her head turned in his direction, but her eyes never opened. "Great medicine," she added softly.

That medicine had to be better than great. Her face had eased, and he was certain she wasn't feeling any pain at the moment. He rested his hand on her seat's headrest, inches from her soft curls. He gave in to the urge to brush them back from her forehead. "Glad Moses could help you," he said, a total understatement.

She touched her tongue to her lips, sighed again. "Me, too," she mumbled.

"You just rest," he whispered, then put the truck into gear. The tires grabbed the pavement, and snow fell gently from the dark sky.

He assumed that Norma and Bingo had some troubles, and he wondered if Faith was in the same boat and if that was why she chose to take off. He barely knew Faith, but he couldn't fathom how any man could not want to protect her.

He concentrated on the road. It was getting hazardously slick from all the snow. He felt the oversize tires lose their grip on the pavement, and he held the steering wheel more tightly, bringing the truck to barely a crawl. He had to figure out the puzzle that was Faith Arden and he had to do it sooner rather than later.

CHAPTER NINE

FAITH WAS IN a strange world. Adam was talking to her, and his voice brushed across her like an errant summer breeze. Pain was there, hovering in the darkness, then she felt a touch, soft and light, skimming across her forehead, barely there. Adam. She just knew it. “Thank you,” she said and her mind drifted deeper.

“For what?” his voice came to her.

“You, just you,” she said, puzzled by her own words.

“You don’t have anyone who’s worried about you?” The question seemed tentative, and she wondered what kind of dream she was in. She heard Adam, felt no barriers to answering the question. A strange dream, she thought. “Just one. That’s all.”

“Who?”

The single word hung there, almost as if

she could reach out and touch it. "Dad," she admitted and felt a terrible pang of need for her father. But it softened right away and she relaxed.

"Where is he?" Adam asked.

"Home."

"Home?"

"Oh, yes." She sighed. "Home." She loved that word. "Home," she said again, hugging it to herself and feeling such a loss that she couldn't bear the sadness.

This seemed a horrible dream. Only her own sobs could be heard, until she felt a touch, then heat all around her, arms holding her, words whispering to her. "It's okay. It's okay."

There was gentleness and caring in each word and it seeped into her soul. She whispered, "I…I need…" She didn't know what she needed, except to stay here forever.

Then tender fingers tipped her face up. "I just want to make things better for you. Tell me what's wrong?"

Wrong? She was confused; she needed to make things right for her father, to obliterate those files and what they said. She was almost afraid she'd told him that. A finger came to rest lightly on her lips. "Please, just tell me," the voice pled.

"I want to."

"What about your dad? Is he okay? Are you okay?"

She felt sadness building again, and she wanted to run away from it all. To go anywhere. She twisted to get free, but the instant she felt the arms around her start to leave her, she panicked and reached out. She didn't understand any of this, but she knew that if he ever let her go, she'd be lost in the darkness. Without him, she would be gone.

ADAM HAD PULLED the truck off the road partly because of the lack of traction and partly because he heard Faith start to cry.

"Don't...don't let me go," she asked unsteadily.

"I won't," he promised and heard her sigh. He knew that the medication was playing havoc with her, but still, she'd answered some questions. He just hadn't expected the emotion that came with them. He'd reached for her, comforting her, hoping he was calming her down. He would stay like that as long as she needed him to.

She shifted and the temptation to kiss her right there and then struck him hard. He fought it, knowing she wasn't herself, that she was too vulnerable like this.

Then Faith touched his face, her fingers skimming along his jaw and back to the nape of his neck. Her warmth seemed everywhere, infusing him, and she came so close to him that the heat of her breath brushed his skin as she whispered on a soft sob, "Don't let me go." He felt her hand tug at him, trying to draw him down to her, and he fought it.

"I won't," he said, and he was rewarded with the shadow of a smile on her full lips. "I won't let you go," he repeated, something being brought to life in him with her nearness and that hint of a smile.

His arm slipped around her more securely, her head nuzzling into his neck, and he closed his eyes so tightly that bright colors exploded behind his lids. *Intense* didn't begin to describe his feelings right then, the conflicts in him almost suffocating. But he held her, felt her relax more and more, and she burrowed even closer against him where his jacket parted.

There was nothing honorable about what

was going through his mind right then, but when she moved back a bit, her face visible, her eyes closed and her breathing even, he allowed himself one pleasure. He bent and pressed his lips to her forehead, then he moved back as carefully as he could.

Honorable? He looked at her, settling against the seat as he eased his arm out from behind her, heard her sigh. Not even close to honorable, he thought with self-loathing. He vowed the next time he kissed this woman, really kissed her, she would want his kiss as much as he wanted hers.

Adam waited until Faith was asleep, never taking his eyes off her as he listened to her soft, even breathing. Her face still held a trace of tears, her lips still parted. He started the truck again and drove away, the street all but obliterated by the snow. A few people were still out, battling the elements, and a sprinkling of cars inched along the street.

Faith had to have been in some state between sleep and reality. When he'd held her, he'd hated the sadness he'd felt in her after she'd mentioned home and her father. A death? A desertion? She ran away? Or simply left? Or was told to go? She settled more, and he exhaled, not realizing until then how involved his emotions had become with this woman.

Adam was startled when his phone rang. They were almost at the inn, but he stopped anyway and answered the call. “Yes?”

It was Chief, and he sounded as if he was out in a storm. “Hey, Adam, got news for ya.”

He kept his eyes on Faith. “What?”

“Got Bingo Sage right here.”

“Where’s here?”

“At the Green Arrow. Got him good. We’re getting in my truck and remembered I didn’t know where you wanted him to go.”

“The hospital. Ask at the E.R. desk for Moses or Merry Brenner and they’ll get him to his son.”

“You got it,” the man said, then he yelled at Bingo, “Just get in the truck, you fool!”

“I owe you, Chief.”

“Yeah, and I’ll take whatever offerings you have when you’re in the neighborhood.”

Adam chuckled. “It’s a deal,” he said and he hung up.

The Sage boy would be okay. With Merry and Moses on his side, they’d sort out the situation at home. Things had a way of working out, he thought as he tore his gaze away from Faith and reached to put the truck in gear, but was stopped when she moaned.

FAITH KNEW she was waking up.

Everything came back in a rush, the migraine, Adam finding her, the E.R., the shot, then the pain fading. But she was still in Adam's truck, and the notion confused her. Not in the hospital, not at the inn. That voice that she'd dreamed of, the kiss on her forehead…had it been real? No, it couldn't have been real, not with Adam.

Carefully, she turned toward the voice and managed to focus on Adam, his features relaying his concern.

He didn't speak, and she felt as if he was waiting for her to say something. Had she imagined or dreamed the parts about the doctor and the shot, then crying and being held? Then kissed? She finally chanced a question. "Are we going to the hospital?"

He shook his head slowly. "No, been there, done that."

So that part hadn't been a dream. "A shot, he gave me a shot?"

"Yes, said it would help the pain, and he gave you some pills to take later."

"Oh." One word was all she could manage as she closed her eyes, unable to even ask about what had happened after that. Maybe if she didn't ask, it would just disappear.

"You don't remember?" he said. There was worry in his tone.

"Yes, of course, but…" No, she couldn't play that off. "I sort of remember. Some things." She wasn't sure what else to say. "We're going to the inn?"

"Yes, but the snow was coming down so hard, I had to pull over for a bit to take a phone call. And then you started coming to."

She'd made a decision to stay out of sight, to keep her distance from the people in town, to do nothing to draw attention to herself until her car was fixed. But she'd landed right in front of a cop who seemed to have a wide streak of the Good Samaritan in him. Obviously she had failed miserably at not getting involved. She pushed herself up a bit, feeling better. The pain had subsided.

"Can we go now?" she asked, badly needing her privacy, a door, a room between her and the world. She was as certain as she could be that the person holding her, comforting her and, yes, kissing her so softly on her forehead had been Adam.

"Sure, of course," he said, "but it's going to be slowgoing. Not much traction out there right now."

She hadn't expected to be so dependent on the kindness of strangers. And he was a stranger, a nice one, an attractive one, but still a stranger and a cop. And he had no idea who was in the truck with him. She was uncomfortable with that and so many other things. He'd been up-front with her ever since they'd met.

"Should we wait a bit longer?" she asked.

"I think so."

"But you have to be somewhere for that boy, don't you?"

He narrowed his eyes. "How did you know that?"

"I can remember some of your conversation...." she said, the words cutting through her consciousness. Adam asking someone about a man with a strange name, whose son was hurt. That hadn't been a dream. The rest hadn't been a dream, either. She remembered his comfort, his arms around her and her need for him.

"You must have heard me talking to my friend on the phone. He's the one who told me where to look for the mother and father."

So up-front with her, as always. Even in the dimness, she was unable to meet his gaze. "Then get me back so you can go," she said.

"I don't have to now. The friend found Bingo and is taking him to be with his son at the hospital."

"Bingo?" she asked distractedly as she stared into the night.

"That's his nickname, and around here nicknames are plentiful, and all of them make sense to someone. The main thing is, Bingo is going to be with his kid when the kid needs him."

Unexpectedly, he reached out and touched her hand. The gesture was both comforting and frightening. Especially when she felt the urge to twine her fingers with his. "Yes," she whispered.

"No one, especially a child, should be alone when they're scared and hurt."

She drew away from his touch and stared straight ahead, uncertain why the sadness from the dream was coming back so forcefully. She was alone. It was her choice, but part of her had wanted her dad with her in the E.R. She could understand how much a child would want and need a parent with them when they were going through frightening things.

"How…how old is the boy?"

"Eight," he answered.

Eight had been a good year for her. She'd made wishes on every star she could see in the heavens, a wish for her father to remarry, so she'd have a mother, and he'd have someone, too. She'd shared that wish with her father when they'd been on the roof of the Chicago town house one hot summer night. She'd spotted a shooting star and he'd told her to make a wish. She had crossed her fingers and said out loud, "I wish for a wife for my dad."

He'd chuckled at that, but it had been a poignant sound. "Honey, I don't need a wife. I had the best, and I was so lucky. Most people never find that one true love. But the ones who do know to cherish it as long as possible and to hold onto the memory forever."

"But, what about me having a mom?" she'd asked without hesitation.

He'd sobered and hugged her. "I didn't realize I was being so selfish. Tell you what," he'd said with all seriousness, "if I find what I had with your mother with someone else, I might give marriage another go."

She'd hugged him back, laughing, figuring he'd find someone and she'd have a mother, and they'd both be happy. But as the years went by, she'd decided that some people only found that love once, and there were no second chances.

One true love. A romantic notion, maybe, but something she'd thought long and hard about. And maybe that was why, as she grew up, she'd never had any serious relationships. Not one of the men she'd dated had qualified as being close to her one true love. She wasn't sure what would happen when that man came into her life, but she knew with a certainty that if he did, she would know who he was right away.

"You sure you're okay?" Adam asked.

"Sure" she said, and though she didn't know why, she added, "Mallory said that you're a Carson."

"Mallory told you that?"

"Yes," she told him and saw the source of the green glow she'd noticed. The florist's had green lights, a green wreath, green everything on the building, its outline twinkling prettily. "And she said that you're with the police."

"Guilty on both charges," he answered and she could feel his eyes on her. "Born a Carson and working in Dallas on the force there."

She took a deep breath and asked, "Why don't you work here?"

"I did for a year, but I ended up in Dallas."

"You're good friends with that man, the cop who stopped me on my way here?"

"John Longbow? Yeah, we've known each other all our lives. He was with me in the police academy and we graduated together."

She closed her eyes tightly. He was so connected in this town, it was a mess. She rubbed at her temple. "Did he tell you about stopping me for speeding?"

"I was in the car with him."

"You were…?"

"He was giving me a ride back to town." He paused, then asked a question she hadn't anticipated. "Does the friend you're traveling with have your car?"

Her car? Her friend? She drew a blank, then she realized what he was asking. "Oh, no, my car broke down."

"And where's your friend?" The question seemed fraught with tension, but she didn't understand why.

"There is no friend. I'm traveling alone."

"Why did you lie to me about leaving town and about being with a friend?"

He distanced himself a bit, moving back to press his back to the door. One hand was draped over the steering wheel, his fingers smoothing the leather with slow circles.

"I didn't lie," she managed. She wanted to say she never lied, but that would be the biggest lie of all. "I thought I was leaving, but my car broke down, and then I thought it was fixed, and it wasn't."

"And the friend?"

She narrowed her eyes to minimize the green Christmas lights flashing across his face. "I didn't know you, and I just thought it was easier to say that than to go into what I'm doing here."

"And what are you doing in Wolf Lake?"

That was a huge slip. She hadn't even thought before she said it. "Getting away for a rest," she ad-libbed with a confidence that startled her. When had lying become so easy for her?"

She had to change the conversation. "And you're a Carson. You never even told me that you're part of that family and probably own most of the area."

He shrugged and his fingers on the leather stilled. "No, just a chunk. It's mostly the Wolf clan that have the land. That comes from my grandfather's people on my mother's side. They moved around, half of them on the res, and the other half, striking out for other places. My grandfather's immediate family stayed close, helping to establish Wolf Lake, and he developed a part of the Wolf family land grant right above the newer ranch where the party was held last night."

"Why didn't you tell me who you are?"

Despite the tension, that brought an easy smile to his face, and even in the green glow, she could see that dimple come to life. "You never asked, and I actually thought you probably knew." He shifted, moving a bit closer, and the smile stayed put. "I am a Carson, but that's where it ends." He motioned a hand in general around them. "This isn't mine, none of it. I work for a living, and I'm only here off and on for visits, like now."

He worked for a living. She bit her lip hard. "So the ranch is…?"

"It started as my grandfather's, and the Carson land came though my mother from him. My mother and father developed the more southern area into the main ranch. My grandfather stayed at the adobe he'd built on about three hundred acres. The rest of his kids, seven in all, spread out to other parts of the land."

"But you left."

"I live in Dallas, I told you, and just came back for the holidays." He exhaled roughly. "No, that isn't completely true. I'm here for the holidays, but I came back because my oldest brother has been going through some things I thought I could help him with."

A cop with the mind-set of a rescuer. He'd helped her and he'd come all the way home to help his brother. "I hope it works out for you, and for him."

"It will," he said almost as if he was assuring himself of that, rather than her. "It will."

He reached for the gearshift. "Let's try moving and see how it goes."

"Fine," she murmured, hoping he could see the road more clearly than she could.

As if Adam read her concern, he touched her hand with his again, closing his fingers around hers and saying softly, "It won't be long. Hang in there." He squeezed her hand slightly before letting it go.

AS THEY PARKED at the inn, Adam's phone rang again. Moses. Adam answered it. "Yes?"

"Where are you?" Moses demanded.

"At the inn. Chief found Bingo and—"

"I know. They're here now and the mother showed up. Hazel found her. But Mallory said Faith was not at the inn yet. Are there problems?"

"Only this snow and the icy roads. We stopped for a bit by the florist's shop and talked." He looked ahead at the lit porch. "We're about to go in now."

"Talked? Faith is okay?"

"Seems to be. That medicine helped a lot."

"What aren't you telling me?"

Faith was listening, so Adam asked, "What do you mean?"

"I know you think she's in trouble and you have to do something about that."

"Okay," he said. "So?"

"So did she ask you to do something about that?"

He really hated the direct way Moses dealt with life and with his friends. "No."

"Then why?"

Adam could have gone into a long explanation about how helping people made him feel good, or how just because he wasn't in uniform didn't mean he couldn't give her a hand. But he didn't. He couldn't. And there was no answer he could get a handle on that he'd believe himself.

He looked at Faith, and the simple truth came. He just wanted to help her. She touched something in him that he hadn't admitted to himself until the kiss. So he did the predictable thing when he was uncomfortable with a question. He met it with one of his own. "Why not?"

"Whatever," Moses said, annoying Adam with that response.

"Yeah, whatever," he muttered.

"Get her inside, and make sure when she

takes the pills I gave her that she eats something."

"Yes, sir."

"Just do it," Moses said and hung up.

Adam stared at the phone, then slipped it into his pocket. He'd walked away from a lot of situations where he could have done some good if he'd made a point of interfering. He'd had to. He could only do so much as a cop, and he wouldn't beat himself up about the rest. But with Faith, it was personal and getting more personal every time he was close to her. He had a gut feeling if he didn't try to help her, and if anything happened to her, he wouldn't forgive himself. That was a fact, and he couldn't and wouldn't hide from it.

CHAPTER TEN

FAITH WAS VERY STILL. She hadn't been watching him talk on the phone after all. Her head was back against the headrest, and her eyes were closed.

"Any better?" Adam asked, worried because she'd been so talkative only moments ago.

"Perfect."

"You're a bad liar," he said, seeing a flush to her skin now and a thin film of perspiration. A single dark curl clung to the dampness on her forehead.

"I'm sorry for this," she murmured thickly.

She was sorry? "Why, did you wish for a migraine?"

She put a hand to her cheek and he saw unsteadiness in the contact. "You needed to help that little boy, and I got in the way."

What happened to the woman who had

interrogated him about being a Carson? Her voice broke on the last few words, and he saw moisture at the corners of her eyes. There was something there, but about her father, not her mother. He didn't think before reaching over to close his hand on hers the way he had before, a move so natural to him that it shocked him. "No, it's resolved now. Chief took care of it. Everything's just fine."

She bit her lip but didn't move away from his touch. "Will he be okay?"

"He's got the best doctor around. He'll be better in no time." Adam drew back, breaking their contact, and he felt as if he'd been set adrift.

"I hope so."

He stared at her, wishing he could read her expression. "Trust me, he'll be okay."

She surprised him by saying, "Thank you," again, in little more than a whisper. He saw her eyes narrow, as if she were trying to focus on him. "You are so…" Her tongue touched her pale lips.

He wanted to repeat her comment, but didn't. Instead, he asked something that had been bugging him since they'd started this talk. "Can I ask you something?"

"Okay." She pronounced the word so that it sounded like two words, *oh* and *kay*.

"When are you actually leaving Wolf Lake?"

She grimaced. "Why?"

"I'm getting whiplash watching you leave, then not leave, then leave, then not leave." He smiled, trying to keep things light, but he really wanted the truth.

Her grimace morphed into a look he'd seen on more than one guilty criminal. "I *was* leaving," she said. "I meant to leave, but things changed. I told you about the stupid car." She sounded almost petulant now. "I have this car that I just bought and it worked fine, then it burned up."

She shifted, looking uncomfortable and embarrassed. He hadn't heard of a car fire in town, and that was something someone would have mentioned. "There was a fire?"

"I was going the first time, but then the car wouldn't start and I smelled something burning. I thought it was a battery, but it was the wiring. It melted. And when I saw you in the coffee shop, I thought I was leaving then, or the next day, but I didn't. And the car still isn't fixed, even though I thought I was going right after the dance." She sped up as she spoke. "And I thought for sure the car would be done by now, but it's not."

Well, at least a part of the puzzle called Faith made sense to him. "So this has all been about your car breaking down?"

"Pretty much," she said, not making any effort to get out of the truck. "I couldn't leave. I wanted to. I needed to. I can't stay here."

"Why?"

"I have to get back."

He frowned at her. "Back where?"

She exhaled harshly. "Just back, okay?"

"To Illinois?"

That brought a fiery look from her that took him aback. She had color now, blotches of red at her cheeks, and her even teeth had trapped her bottom lip. "What?" she said in a tight voice.

"I thought your car had Illinois plates on it," he said reasonably.

"So that means I'm from Illinois, I guess?" she said, sitting up straighter. "But I told you I bought the car used, and this all makes me wonder what sort of cop you are."

Whoa, he was losing control of everything

here. "Just go ahead and say whatever you need to say, then I'll get you inside," he offered. Enough was enough. She needed to be in bed.

"I have to ask you something, and I don't want you to think I'm crazy," she said in a breathy voice.

He didn't want this. He'd already had his control tested once this evening. Now the look in those eyes was unsettling. There was an urgency in her gaze, a need for him to let her ask her question. He finally relented.

"Did I… Did you and I… Did you kiss me, or did I…?"

Her distress was almost his undoing. He wanted to say that nothing had happened, nothing important, but that was an incredible lie, at least for him. "You were upset and talking about your dad, and I thought maybe your dad had passed or something."

"No," she said abruptly. "No, he didn't pass. He's okay. He will be okay."

"Then I'm sorry." As good as he was at being able to read people, to prove his hunches correct, every time he thought he had a handle on this woman, he was all wrong.

"What else did I say?" she asked in a slow,

measured way. She was rubbing at her temple again.

"Nothing much, not really."

She seemed to be figuring something out, then took him aback when she asked, "I told you I'm between jobs, didn't I?"

He watched her closely. "You didn't say what your job was or what you're looking for in employment."

"I take care of money." She stopped rubbing her temple. "Boring stuff."

"You're in banking?" he prodded gently.

"Oh, I guess so."

"And you need to get back to find a job or something?"

"Yes," she said and glanced out the windshield. "We're here?" she asked, seemingly surprised that they were sitting in front of the inn.

"Yes, we are. And you need to get out of the cold."

He left the truck, going around to her door quickly. He wondered about calling Moses. She seemed confused, probably because of the medication. He wasn't at all sure it was safe to just leave her here.

Adam pulled open the passenger door.

"Faith?" She seemed to shiver at the sound of her name, and then she turned and looked at him. "Do you want me to take you back to the hospital?"

"No," she said, fumbling to undo her seat belt. She gripped the armrest on the door with one hand and the door frame with the other, moving slowly on the seat, one foot coming down to find the step for support. Adam wouldn't mind carrying her if he had to. But she was making it on her own, only taking his hand when she stepped down onto the snowy ground.

They went into the inn, and as they pushed the door open, the heat hit them. Adam barely had time to swing the door shut before Mallory burst out of the back area.

"There you are!" she said, heading toward them. "I was getting so worried." She was carrying a small tray in her hands as she came to them, acknowledging Adam with a glance and then Faith. "Moses called and said you'd left there a long time ago." She held up the tray that had a mug of clear tea, a dish with crackers and some sliced fruit in a bowl. "He said to make sure you eat something, even if it's just the crackers." Mallory motioned with her head toward the stairs. "Lead the way and let's get you settled."

Faith cast Adam a grateful look, then she followed Mallory.

He watched Faith go, wanting to join the procession to make sure she got to the top safely. "Mallory, the medication John gave her is making her a bit disoriented."

"Moses told me about it and to make sure she got food. That'll take care of it. Don't you worry."

"Okay," he said, but didn't make a move to go.

FAITH GLANCED BACK at Adam still standing at the bottom of the stairs. She managed to make her way along the upper hallway, and Mallory passed her to get her door open.

By the time she stepped into the room, Mallory had the light on, the bed turned down and the tray on the nightstand. In the distance, Faith heard the door chime and she knew Adam had gone.

Mallory pushed the tray closer to the bed. "Do you need help getting undressed?"

"Oh, no, I'm okay," she said, although she

felt fairly weak. She slipped off her jacket, and Mallory helped her tug off her boots.

"Moses said he gave you pills for later?" she asked.

Faith pointed to her jacket. "They're in my pocket, I think."

Mallory searched the pockets, but came up empty. "Nothing there."

Faith tried to think. "Oh, no, I must have left them in Adam's truck." She started to get up, but Mallory stopped her.

"Oh, no, you don't. I'll go see if I can stop him before he leaves."

She was back in less than a minute, holding the foil packets of pills. "Good luck. He was on his phone in the truck, so I caught him." She put the packets on the nightstand. "Moses said you should take them in three hours, not any sooner. And don't forget to eat a bit with the pill, okay?"

"Yes," Faith said, thankful that Mallory cared so much. "I'm really tired," she admitted.

Mallory nodded, then crossed the room. "Call if you need me," she said as she reached for the doorknob.

Faith watched her and heard herself ask, "Was Adam always this helpful?"

Mallory looked startled. "What?"

"He seems to be a natural do-gooder, helping me like this and trying to help that little boy. And his brother, too," she added, hearing her words getting a bit thick with emotion.

Mallory smiled. "He's a natural-born helper of people. It's an occupational thing, I think. Most cops are basically do-gooders," she said. "Now get some sleep."

"Thanks," she said and watched the door close.

She eased back onto the bed, into the soft comforter, and measured her feelings. The pain was there, but the worst of it was gone. She didn't bother getting undressed, but shifted carefully on the bed to rest against the headboard.

She breathed evenly, willing her muscles to relax, trying not to think about anything other than getting to sleep.

Tomorrow she'd be better and her car might be fixed. She could leave. She could head off to somewhere, a place where she wouldn't make the mistake of getting involved with anyone. She exhaled. Involved? That was an odd dream she'd had in the truck.

She didn't know if Adam had held her and reassured her or if that had been the product of wishful thinking on her part or plain need. She'd mentioned her father, he'd told her. She felt her breath come in a sharp intake. He'd never answered her completely about what else she might have told him. She pushed that away, letting the medication draw her farther from reality as it kept masking the pain. The only important thing right now had to be that she got better and that she could leave and be in a place where no one knew her. She couldn't have ties like she did to the people around here, people who belonged. She didn't.

So little had gone the way she'd planned since she'd left. But then she hadn't planned on landing in a town like Wolf Lake or meeting anyone like Adam. She also hadn't planned on finding that information in the files linked to her father.

She scrunched her eyes more tightly shut as she willed herself to go to sleep. Then Mallory's words came to her out of nowhere, something about Adam being a rescuer. *It's an occupational thing...cops are like that...* the woman had said, and Faith moaned softly.

Yes, worst of all, the man was a cop. She'd let a cop help her. She had to be insane to not get away from Adam as quickly as possible. She sighed heavily. The worst thing of all was that she didn't want to get away from him. She didn't want him to leave her. But that was exactly what had to happen. The burning behind her eyes faded as sleep finally enveloped her.

ADAM WASN'T READY to go back to the guesthouse at the ranch. He remembered John was called back to work tonight, and so he changed his route to go by the police station. The building looked the same as it had in his day. A metal roof over a long rectangular structure fashioned in chipped stucco faded to a terrible shade of pink. It had been a local joke about it being pink when Adam was a kid, and he was sure today's kids had their own jokes about it.

He pulled his truck in between two parked cruisers, then headed inside through the still-falling snow. The front desk was vacant, but he caught the smell of coffee and the sound of voices coming from a corridor. He strode down to the first open door and looked inside the chief of police's office.

John was behind his desk, his booted feet resting on the papers strewn across the top. Bobby Ray, one of the small crew of deputies, had his back to the only window in the space and his arms crossed on his chest.

"I could have robbed you blind," Adam said as he entered the room. "No one's at the desk or anywhere out there."

John pointed at Bobby Ray. "Get on out there, Officer, and protect the pencils, but be especially vigilant with that vending machine that has pistachios in it. I hate it when I get a taste for them and they've all be stolen."

Bobby Ray barked a laugh at that, nodded to Adam, said, "Good to see you, sir," then went past him and swung the door shut behind him.

"Done with your call out?" Adam asked as he sank down into one of the chairs by the desk.

"Yeah, came after you left. Turned out to be routine, though, so I headed back here for a bit." Jon tugged the bolo tie at the collar of his uniform loose and popped the top two buttons of the shirt. "So I'm here, and you're here."

"Thank Hannah again for dinner. She's a great cook."

"That she is," John said. "You mentioned you were going to call Robert to find out more about Jack's idea of moving there. How'd it go?"

Adam shook his head. "It didn't. I got to thinking that Jack's got to take care of things in his own way. I'll call Robert after the New Year and feel him out, but I don't want to intrude right now."

"Good plan," John said, then slapped the papers on the desk with the flats of his hands and sat up straighter. "I heard all about the rescue missions you've been running since you came back into town."

Adam shook his head as he unbuttoned his jacket. "What in the—"

"Talked to Moses about an hour ago and heard about Brandon Sage, then the doc ratted you out about the lady. The whole town knows about you coming back for Jack. But it's the lady I was interested in."

"Why are you interested in her?"

He sat back, clasping his hands behind his

head and putting his boots back up on the desktop. "You know I saw you at the party alone with her. Then you were dancing with her. What I want to know is, did you figure her out?"

"Not even close," he admitted on a gruff chuckle. "Why do you want to know?"

"Why wouldn't I?" he asked. "I stopped her for speeding, merely warned her to slow down. I told you she seemed upset, and the next thing I know, you're with her, and now you've been running her around town for medical help after you ate at my table and never even mentioned her." He shrugged. "It got my curiosity going."

The town was a hotbed of gossip, always had been. He exhaled and stared at a spot above John's head, in the vicinity of one of the many certificates he'd earned at the shooting range. "You're the one who thought she was upset or maybe afraid." He met John's patient gaze and filled him in on his short story with Faith. He finally admitted that he'd made contact at the party because he thought she was attractive and then re-alized there was something going on with her. "I thought she looked shocked or scared when she saw you in the doorway."

"She looked uneasy," John amended.

"At the least. Since then, we've talked a bit, and although she won't tell me much about herself, I'm almost certain that she's running, not sure from what, obviously not from anything good. I offered to help, to listen if she needed to talk, but she isn't having any part of that idea."

"She's pretty determined if she won't talk to you," he said with a grin. "Most women crumble when you smile and flash your Carson dimple."

Adam waved that off. "I know her name's Faith Arden, and she claimed there was no one to call when she was in the hospital with Moses. She's probably from Illinois, from the license on the car, but maybe not, and she gets migraines." He wouldn't go into her crying when she mentioned home or how the look in her blue eyes cut right through him when she looked so incredibly sad. He certainly didn't admit to John that he'd wanted nothing better than to kiss her and not stop. That was gut-wrenching.

John listened, then glanced at the clock on

the wall. "Midnight. This Cinderella has to get home." He stood and stretched. "Sounds like you do know quite a bit about her."

Adam spread his hands palms up. "Sure. Add all that to a nickel and two dimes and you'll get a quarter."

"Well, add this to your list. She's from Rockford, Illinois. I remember that from the license she gave me at the stop. Also, she's twenty-six, going to be a year older in a few days," he said as he put on his heavy jacket. "Mallory told Bobby Ray that her guest stays in her room most of the time, seems to be doing work on the computer and her car's over at Dent's. The electrical circuits were fried."

"You're just a mine of information, aren't you?" Why had he called Connor, his partner, instead of just waiting for John to get the facts? And of course the car was at Dent's. There were only a couple of mechanics in town, and Dent was the best. He stood, too. "What about the people she bought that car from?"

"I checked there, after the fact, actually, after I talked to Moses tonight. Found out they're an older couple, downsizing and moving to Florida, but on some cruise for four weeks, so they're out of contact."

"Anything else?"

"The only reason she went to your family party was so Mallory wouldn't have to go alone. She didn't want to go, to be around people, but she did it for Mallory, who's pretty much a stranger to her. Now, tell me something?"

"What?"

"What's your guess about what's happening with her?"

"I've got one or two, but nothing I'd want to bet on. And she's not talking about it at all."

"But you're going to find out, aren't you?"

He answered immediately. "Yes, I'm going to try."

"That's why you're such a good cop. You're like a dog with a bone when you get onto something."

Adam shook his head as he redid his jacket. "Now I'm a dog, huh?"

"No, just a born worrier," John said with a grin.

Adam followed him out, crossed to the truck through the falling snow, while John went for his own car parked off to one side. He opened the door, calling to his friend, "John?"

"What?"

"Can I come by in the morning and use your computer?"

"Sure. I'll be in around noon."

Adam waved a thank-you, then got into the truck and headed out to the ranch.

Faith Arden, from Rockford, Illinois, almost twenty-seven and alone in the world. Meager information that didn't include incredibly blue eyes, midnight curls and porcelain skin. Or that she felt soft and warm in his arms when they'd danced. Or fragile when she'd been crying.

He flipped on the car radio, turned up the volume of an '80's music station and let the noise drown out his thoughts while he drove through the snowy night. But it didn't blot out anything about Faith. Memories would surely fade, but he wasn't sure they would ever be completely forgotten.

CHAPTER ELEVEN

WHEN FAITH WOKE the next morning, feeling as if she had been hit by a truck, she didn't even think about getting out of bed. She took two of the pills the doctor had given her, washed them down with water, then nibbled on the end of an energy bar. She used her cell phone to make a call to Dent that only proved frustrating, since her car still wasn't done. The wires he'd put in were working, but he was still waiting on delivery of a part to complete the job. She didn't care what it was; she just wanted the car done.

She hung up, knowing she was here for another day at least, so she lay back down and pulled the covers up over her head. She stayed very still as she waited for the medication to kick in and give her some relief.

She tried not to think about anything or anyone. But that was impossible. Flashes of the night before came to her and she pushed them away as quickly as she could. But one kept coming back, one of Adam, though she realized it had to be wrong. He'd never held her to him, never brushed his lips across her forehead. Never. Surely she would know for sure if any of that had ever happened.

"Stupid," she muttered. But it came again, the safety she'd felt in the dream, the shocking easiness with which she had leaned into Adam. Not a memory, not real. She rolled onto her side, and as the throbbing started to diminish, she felt sleep tugging at her again.

There might have been a knock on the door and someone saying something, or she dreamed it. She didn't know.

"She's so alone. I want to help, that's all." More words drifted around her before fading away.

Faith eased her eyes open a slit, not sure if she'd slept or not. The room was quiet. She assessed her headache and was pleased that the pain was barely there.

Footsteps on the stairs meant someone was coming closer, then she caught sight of Mallory stepping cautiously into the room. She smiled as soon as she realized Faith was awake. "Well, hello, there. Good to see you're up."

"Sort of."

Mallory came to the bed carrying a small tray with a pitcher of fresh water and a glass on it. She poured the water and offered the drink to Faith. "You might need this."

Faith reached for the water, sipped the coolness, then handed it back to Mallory, who was hovering over her. "Did I sleep very long?" she asked.

"Awhile. When I came to check on you, you didn't answer and then Moses came, and he said you were just in a deep sleep from the medication. You were exhausted from everything."

She could feel the weariness lifting. She so appreciated Mallory's kindness, Moses's, too, and…Adam's. "Thanks for being concerned," she said.

"No problem." She studied Faith after she set the water glass on the nightstand. "You're still pale, but you look ever so much better. How do you feel?"

"The pain is pretty much gone."

Mallory smiled down at her. A holly-wreath necklace woven with tiny red and green blinking lights accented a deep red cabled sweater she was wearing. "That's good to hear."

"I need to rent the room for another night," she said, knowing even if the car was finally ready, she wasn't in any condition to drive right away. "I haven't paid to stay any longer than this morning," she said. "Last night was crazy with the E.R. and things. I haven't had a migraine like that since college."

"It was crazy, but your hospital experience was two nights ago," Mallory said without blinking.

Faith frowned. "What?"

"You slept all day yesterday and most of today." Mallory glanced at the nightstand clock. "It's almost three in the afternoon."

"What's the date?" she asked, confused and vaguely afraid of the answer.

"It's three days to Christmas, December twenty-second."

Faith exhaled. "Are you sure?"

"Absolutely."

She closed her eyes to hide the panic she was afraid would show. She had no idea what had been going on here, let alone back in Chicago. December 22. Her birthday. She took a deep breath and said, "Let me get my wallet, and I'll pay what I owe you and take care of tonight."

"Don't worry about that now," Mallory said, but Faith motioned to her purse on the chair by the door.

"Please, I need to pay you. My wallet's in my purse under my jacket. Could you get it for me?"

When Mallory handed the purse to Faith, she immediately felt that something wasn't right. Then she knew. It was the weight. It was far too light. She pulled it open and looked inside. Her heart lurched. Her wallet wasn't there. She turned the purse over and dumped the contents out onto the rumpled comforter. A pen, a map of Texas, a few pieces of makeup, tissues, the receipts for the payments she'd made on this room, the envelope with the picture her dad had given her and the box with her bracelet. But no wallet.

She quickly looked around at the dresser and side tables, then over by the computer. She couldn't see it. "My wallet. I had it. I..." She remembered grabbing it when she'd left for the room, then having it in Adam's truck, on the seat by her. She'd used it when she'd paid the bill at the hospital. She closed her eyes tightly, trying to envision getting back in the truck, and she thought she remembered it being there along with the pills.

"Could you see if my wallet fell out of my purse on the chair?" she asked Mallory, trying to hide her growing panic.

It took less than a minute for Mallory to say, "It's not there."

It had been on the truck seat, or maybe she was imagining she'd seen it. Either way, it was gone, and so was a huge chunk of her cash, not to mention her real driver's license along with a few credit cards.

What if she'd dropped it, and what if someone found it and went through it to find information about the owner? Sickness rose in her throat. She spoke to Mallory with as much calmness as she could muster. "My wallet isn't here and I think I left it at the hospital."

Mallory held up a hand. "Just stay put and I'll be right back."

When Mallory returned minutes later, she said, "I spoke to the nurse who was there when you checked out, and you definitely left with it in your lap in the wheelchair with the pills. They checked with security, in case someone found it in the hospital, or in case it fell when you were getting into the truck, but nothing's been turned in."

Faith tried to think what to do, and then her world crashed with a thud. Adam, his truck. "I…I must have left it in Adam's truck, but I don't remember." If Adam found it and opened it… She willed herself not to scream in frustration. "I have to get to him."

Mallory shook her head. "First, let's check around downstairs in case it fell out when you got back."

Faith hadn't thought of that, and she let hope grow as Mallory hurried off. The chime sounded, and the door closed. After what seemed like forever, Mallory came back inside and up to the room. She looked cold, rubbing her arms and stomping her feet. "Boy, it's freezing out there," she said. "But no wallet. I'm so sorry."

"Thanks for trying," Faith said and made some quick calculations in her head. She had enough in her suitcase to pay Mallory, and probably enough to pay Dent for the car repairs, but after that she'd be nearly broke. There was no way, without leaving a trail, that she could get money out of any of her other accounts. "I can still pay you now."

Mallory scoffed, "Don't worry about that now. It's more important to find your wallet."

Faith sat forward. Surely after two days, Adam would have found it. If he opened it, which anyone would to figure things out, and if he looked through it, there was no way he wouldn't know who she really was, short of a miracle. The one man who could destroy her life had it in his hands right now. She had to contact him.

As if Mallory read her mind, she said, "I have Adam's cell-phone number downstairs. Do you want me to get it for you? Or I could drive you out to the Carson ranch so you can talk to him?"

Mallory had already done so much for her, Faith couldn't imagine asking Mallory to drive her out there. Besides, it would be easier to contact Adam by phone. Who knew? She might need to get her car from Dent and leave without ever seeing the wallet again. "The phone number, please," she said as she dropped her hands and sank back against the headboard again. "It's faster." *And safer,* she added to herself. One more chat with Adam, then that was it.

Mallory came back with a number written on a slip of paper topped with the inn's logo. "I knew I had it," she said as Faith took the paper from her.

Faith entered the number into her cell phone and hit Send. There was no ring before there was a click, then Adam's recorded voice saying, "I'm not available, but if this is an emergency, please hang up and dial 911. If you want to talk, just leave a message."

She hesitated, heard the beep. "Adam, it's Faith Arden. I just needed to ask if by any chance you found my wallet in your truck. If you could call me at the inn, I would really appreciate it."

She closed the phone and laid it on the bed beside her. "It went right to voice mail."

"I can still take you out there," Mallory offered quickly.

"Oh, no, I'll wait for him to call," she said. Or for Dent to call and say the car was ready.

Faith glanced at the window, where gray light was peeking through the narrow opening between the curtain panels. The longer the wallet was gone, the more chance there was of disaster. Waiting would be so hard, but if it wasn't at the hospital or outside, it was either gone forever or with Adam.

Mallory obviously sensed the growing distress in Faith. "Don't worry. You'll make yourself sick again. If it's still at the hospital, the staff will find it, and if it's with Adam, it couldn't be in a safer place."

Faith looked up at Mallory. "I guess."

She chuckled softly. "Hey, what's more safe than a cop finding your wallet? And a great cop at that."

"Yes, he is, isn't he?"

"You got lucky, I think."

Faith heard the words, understood the words and barely kept from flinching. Lucky?

She couldn't just sit here while Adam might already know about her, already be in touch with the police in Chicago or with the federal prosecutor. The worst-case scenario could already be in motion. Her course of action was crystal clear. She was going to get her things together as soon as Mallory left, figure out her money situation, then try to get out of here in one piece…alone.

The nausea was growing, and she pulled

back the covers. "Thanks, Mallory, for everything. But right now, I really need a shower," she said as she stood, heading to the bathroom, surprisingly steady on her feet.

"Okay, I'll let you know if I hear anything from anyone, including Adam."

Under the stream of hot water in the shower, Faith tried to think, tried to plan, and she told herself not to expect the worst, but just make sure she got out of there as soon as she could. She thought of calling Dent while she dried off, but pushed that away. She needed to go there and speak to him in person.

When she was dressed in a heavy sweater, fresh jeans and her boots, she took a few dollars out of her remaining bankroll, grabbed her jacket, her cell phone and the room key.

She had a glimmer of hope as she left her room. If Adam had her wallet, he would have found it two days ago, but he hadn't done a thing about it that she knew of. Why wouldn't he bring it to her, ask for an explanation, go from there? Because he was figuring out how to handle her arrest. Him and John Longbow.

She shivered, pushing that awful idea away. On to her first priority. Her car.

She set off for Dent's.

ADAM FELT FRUSTRATED as he sat in the police station behind John's desk and stared at the computer. No one could walk on this earth and not leave a trail at all. But Faith Arden had no trail. Nothing in Illinois, nothing in any other jurisdiction he could search on John's computer. No wonder Connors hadn't found anything under that name, either.

John had left an hour ago, going to make rounds while Adam searched. Now Adam was done. Frustration didn't sit well with him. He wasn't used to coming up with absolutely nothing to show for his time doing a background search. As far as the criminal world was concerned, no one by that name had been an offender or a victim in the past year, or owned a home, a car or even owed library fines.

He put on his leather jacket, his Stetson and left the office, passing Bobby Ray behind the front desk. "Tell John I came up with a goose egg," he said and kept on going.

"Yes, sir," the young deputy called after him.

Adam stepped out into the late-afternoon chill. The sky was gray, but no snow, except for the icy remnants from the storm that had passed through two nights ago. He'd heard that Brandon Sage was doing well, and Jack had called again to let Adam know he was coming back soon. No one knew what that meant. To pack for good or to stay? They'd have to wait.

He got into the truck, turned it on and switched the heater to full blast. Faith's condition wasn't as easily summed up as Brandon's or Jack's, at least not for him. He'd been by the inn two or three times, once actually going up to her room with Moses when he'd insisted on seeing her for himself. She'd been sleeping, her skin cool to his touch, and the sight of her had knotted his stomach.

He'd gone back again, but didn't go up. He'd asked Mallory about her, heard that she was doing okay, just sleeping a lot, and today he'd stayed away. He'd never felt the protectiveness for anyone that he did for Faith, apart from his family. The feeling was focused and intense. And it hadn't lessened with time.

He put the truck into gear and intended to

go back to the ranch, but Bobby Ray came out of the station and jogged over to him.

"What's going on?"

"Sorry, sir," the deputy said, offering him the cordless phone. "A call for you. I thought you'd need to take it."

Adam felt his chest tighten, not sure what to expect when he put the phone to his ear. But his first thought was of Faith. Maybe something had happened to her? "Hello?"

He was surprised to hear his mother on the other end of the line. "Oh, Adam, thank goodness. Your phone's dead or turned off."

He pulled it out of his jacket pocket and realized he hadn't charged it. "It's dead," he said. "What's wrong?"

"It's your dad."

His stomach clenched. He'd heard those words more than once over the years, but this time he knew that he hadn't been stopped in Wolf Lake, that John hadn't brought him in to let him sober up before calling the family to get him. John would have contacted him right away.

"What happened?"

"He's sick. He's en route to the hospital. I'm just leaving now."

"What happened?"

"I'm not sure. He was over at the Yardley's place in Crestline—you know the bank manager at the branch over there—and they said he got short of breath and disoriented."

"I'm on my way."

"Moses is waiting for him. I'm okay and I don't need you here, but I wanted you to know."

He'd never bought that in the past, and he wouldn't buy it now. "I'll see you in ten."

Bobby Ray was still standing in the cold waiting on him with no jacket on. Adam quickly hung up, handed the phone back. "Tell John that my father's in the hospital," he said and roared away from the station.

Adam was at the hospital in record time. The nurse at the urgent-care unit buzzed the security doors open for him to go through without asking him anything. She obviously knew why he was there.

He'd barely got inside when Moses appeared from behind some curtains into the aisle, almost colliding with him. Adam caught a glimpse of his father through the slight parting in the curtains. An intern and nurse were taking his vitals and asking him questions. Herbert Carson looked as if he was stunned, and Adam could hear how rapid and shallow his breathing was. The intern snapped an oxygen mask over his dad's face, pushing up the sleeves of his shirt.

"I knew you'd get here fast once Lark found you," Moses said as he reached around Adam to shut the curtains.

"What's happening?"

Moses folded his arms on his chest. "Believe it or not, I don't know. He just got here, and there are a lot of tests I need to run."

"What do you think is happening?" Adam asked abruptly, his frustration and worry obvious in his tone.

But John was patient. "Anything from a full MI to a—"

"English," Adam said, cutting him off.

"A heart attack, a myocardial infarction or something as simple as indigestion or even an anxiety attack. I don't know yet. With his background, it's hard to tell at first."

Adam turned, taking a long breath, and saw his mother coming through the security doors. She headed right for him, her face wet with tears, and she silently went into his hug, which lasted until she chose to move back.

When he looked down at her, she was controlled, or at least wasn't crying anymore. "They need to do tests and stabilize him," he told her. He didn't want her to hear anything about a heart attack, not unless she had to.

His mother trusted Moses as much as he did, and she moved to touch the doctor's arm. "Please, take care of him."

"Of course I will," Moses said. "This is going to take time, and you can't be with him. Please, go get some coffee and try to stay calm. I'll get back to you as soon as I know anything."

Reluctantly Adam and his mother walked to the waiting room. He looked at the TV on the wall in the corner and he had a flashback to waiting for Faith in the same spot. He hadn't been in this hospital for years, not even to see Moses, and now he'd been here twice in three days, and not for any happy visits.

He stared blankly at the TV, letting his mind recall the past couple of days, then he wished he hadn't. Memories of some things could be so potent. The feeling of Faith in his arms, her boldness, her braveness, having been so sick. He stood abruptly, looked at his watch and realized they'd been sitting there an hour.

He told his mother he'd get them coffee and be right back. But when he returned to the waiting room, his mother was gone. The nurse on duty pointed to the doors and he was buzzed in. Next he saw Moses outside his father's cubicle.

He couldn't read Moses's expression as he hurried over to him, but he did hear his mother sobbing behind the curtain. "What's going on?"

"Hey, hey," Moses said, his hand on Adam's arm. "It's okay. He's okay. She's just relieved and happy."

He exhaled, took a moment, then asked, "What happened to him?"

"Believe it or not, he had an anxiety attack. I gave him some medication, and although a few tests still aren't back, I'm sure it's not anything more than stress and worry."

Adam exhaled harshly. "I thought…"

Even though he didn't finish that thought, Moses knew exactly what he had been going to say. "No, no alcohol involved. Nothing like that. He's doing well on that front. This seems to be just plain old-fashioned nerves, unless the tests show something I'm missing. My bet is they won't."

"He'll be okay?"

"He will be if he takes care of himself. He needs time to just relax for a while."

Adam automatically felt less uneasy. "You know Dad's pretty stubborn. He won't do anything he doesn't want to do."

"He will do what he's told," his mother said in a raised voice.

Adam parted the curtains just enough to see his father's arms around his mother, who was lying on his chest. She was smiling. "You'd better listen to her, Dad."

"He will," Lark said softly. "He will."

Adam pulled back, closing the curtains. He and Moses walked beyond the security doors. As they closed behind them, Adam said simply, "Thank you."

Moses laid his hand on Adam's shoulder. "Hey, I'd do anything for your family."

Adam nodded. "Same here."

Moses slapped his shoulder, started to turn to go back, but stopped and addressed Adam. "Did Faith Arden get ahold of you?"

That question broadsided him. "Is *she* okay?"

"Seems to be, but Mallory called me, said that the lady lost her wallet somewhere and thought it could be here. It's not, but she said she'd contact you to see if she left it in your truck."

"I haven't seen any wallet in the truck."

"That's too bad. I think you were her last hope."

He felt helpless and hated it. Maybe he could check for her or do something. "Could you tell Mom to call if she needs me?"

"Sure." Moses nodded. "Take care."

Adam left the hospital, turned in the direction of the inn and drove through the gathering dusk. Her wallet. He knew the feeling of losing one. He'd done it more than once, and it had been a real inconvenience every time. He suspected that Faith losing her wallet would be a lot more than a mere inconvenience.

He slowed when he thought he recognized Faith on the street. After his mistakes when he'd thought he'd seen her before, he didn't believe it was her until he pulled abreast of her. It was Faith striding down the sidewalk, past the general store, her head down, her pace almost qualifying as a slow run.

He went by, pulled into a parking spot ahead of her and got out of the truck. But she crossed the street before his boots hit the ground, and he took off after her, calling out to her as he went. “Faith! Hey, Faith, stop!”

He could have sworn she paused when he said her name, but she didn’t stop. She acted as if she hadn’t heard anything and sped up as he came along behind her. When he almost reached her, he called out again, “Faith, stop!” and this time he knew she’d heard him. Still, she didn’t stop. He got close enough to reach out, grab at her arm and finally pull her to a stop. She spun around, breaking the contact, facing him with wide eyes.

She didn’t turn away, but stood her ground, breathing hard, and even across the three feet that buffered them from each other, he could tell she was shaking. He took a step toward her, afraid she might run, only to be rewarded by her remaining where she was.

She seemed scared, and why was she practically running? He looked around, certain he’d see somebody coming after her, but he only saw tourists and townspeople going about their business.

"Who are you trying to get away from?" he finally asked, focusing back on her.

She stunned him when she said one word. "You."

CHAPTER TWELVE

FAITH COULD HAVE STOOD there and cried, she felt so drained. She'd heard Adam calling out to her, and she'd run. Why? If he knew all about her, if he was there to take her to the authorities, running was a stupid thing to do. And if he knew nothing, her actions were even more stupid. But she'd been frightened by his voice suddenly behind her. Now he thought someone had been chasing her, some crazed person, when all the while she'd been the one crazed.

He was so obviously a cop that she couldn't figure out how she hadn't guessed it all on her own. His eyes were on her, his attention seemingly centered on her, yet she could tell he was sizing up the street looking for the culprit that didn't exist. And she had no doubt that he'd throw himself in front of her if someone came to hurt her.

"Me?" he asked,

"Not you. I meant, I thought someone was..." She didn't know how to justify what she'd just done without sounding even stranger. So she started walking slowly in the direction she had been running. Back to the inn.

Her meeting with Dent had upset her, and then Adam was there, shouting at her to stop, like on some bad cop show. She couldn't even smile at that. It could have been real. Very real.

She hugged herself as she walked. The car wasn't going to be done tomorrow. She'd be lucky if it was done before Christmas. What a birthday, she thought, one she'd work to forget. Adam caught up to her and matched her stride for stride.

She darted him a glance, then kept her eyes on where her boots were hitting the weathered path through the snow. When he spoke, she missed her step and had to do a double hitch to keep going without falling on her face. "Moses said you're looking for your wallet."

She concentrated on putting one foot in front of the other. "Yes," she said, thankful her voice sounded reasonably normal, despite her nerves.

"I haven't see it anywhere, but I'm sure someone will turn up with it."

The inn was only two blocks ahead. She tried not to give any hint at the relief she felt that he hadn't had her wallet all this time. If she never got it back, she was thankful it hadn't fallen into his hands. She fought the urge to walk faster, but just kept up the pace that Adam was matching. "I hope so," she said.

"Trust me, most people around here who might find it will do everything they can to get it back to its owner."

She didn't stop. "I'm sure they will," she murmured, still reeling from the figure Dent had given her to get the car finished. If she didn't find her wallet, she was going to have to use almost all of her remaining cash to bail her car out and then pay Mallory. She'd been raised with money and made good money at her work, or, at least, had made good money. But right then she fully understood what it meant to be broke.

"How are you feeling?" he asked as they approached the inn.

Horrible, tired and worried. But she didn't say any of that. "I'm okay. The headache is gone."

"I can't believe you could even run like that," he said. "Especially in this miserable cold."

She told him the truth. "I went to the garage to check on my car. Dent said it's not going to be ready for a bit." She grimaced.

"You're safe. Dent's good at what he does and he's honest to a fault."

"And you know him, and he's an old friend from back in the day?"

"Good guess. Yes, he is, and his dad had the garage and gas station from the start, then passed it on to Dent five years ago when he retired."

They were at the inn, and Faith saw the huge motorcycle with the red, white and blue adornments sitting under its cover where her car had once sat. Willie G. must be back, and Adam was still talking.

"Dent's the best there is in town."

"Good to know," she said and was shocked when her stomach growled. She pressed a hand to her middle and shrugged. "I guess I need to get some food."

"I was going to get something before heading back to the ranch. Want to share a table with me?"

If this had been a normal time in her life, she would have loved to do that, but nothing was normal for her anymore. Especially the effect this man had on her, and it got more intense every time they met. She'd run from him, for Pete's sake. How could she sit down to eat with a cop? "No, I don't think so, but thanks."

"My treat," he said quickly and she understood that he thought she was broke since her wallet went missing. Not that that particular scenario wasn't uncomfortably close to her reality at the moment.

"No, I couldn't," she said.

He smiled and gently put the tip of his forefinger to her chin and tilted it up. "Come on. You need food, and I don't need to eat alone," he said as her gaze met his dark eyes. He urged her to agree. "You'd be doing me a favor. I hate eating by myself." Right then, the smile touched his whole face, and she admitted that he wasn't fighting fair, not when he had that dimple in his arsenal.

She was hungry, and no one liked eating

alone. After what he'd done for her, any way she looked at his offer, she owed him that much. And she was worn-out from going over and over what she'd done, losing her wallet with everything in it and trying to think where to go from here. She needed a break, any kind of a break. "I guess I could, if I can get back early. I'm still really tired."

"Thank you," he said, then drew back. "Let's get going."

She glanced at the inn, certain she should be going inside, up to her room and locking the door so she could sort out her future. But that was the last thing she actually wanted to do right then. She wanted to have dinner with Adam and forget for a few hours before she had to face the mess her life had become.

"Just give me a few minutes to freshen up, then we can go."

"Go ahead and I'll bring the truck over here."

"Okay," she agreed.

He took off down the street, and she watched him jog away until he disappeared into the crowd of holiday shoppers. She turned and hurried inside and up to her room, but this time she wasn't locking the door and staying put. She changed her sweater for a yellow silk shirt, pushed some money into her pocket, then got her jacket and headed back downstairs.

Willie G. appeared from the back area, saw her and smiled. "I heard you've been sick, pretty lady, but you look darn good to me."

"Thanks," she said. "I'm fine. You visiting Mallory?"

"Thought I was, but she got a better offer and I'm staying here to cover for her so she can get out for a bit." As she got to the door, he asked, "You going out, too?"

"For a bit," she called back over her shoulder, darting outside.

Adam was there, leaning against the front fender of his truck, arms folded across his chest, his Stetson low over his face. The sight of him came close to taking her breath away. It was ridiculous, she thought, that one person could affect her so intensely. But she kept watching him, a smile shadowing his lips.

"Ready?"

She nodded.

"Okay, let's go," he said as he led the way around to the passenger door.

He opened it for her, but stepped closer and said, "What's that?" He was crouched down, hidden by the partially opened door. Then he rose slowly to his feet, staring at something he had in his hands.

She followed the direction of his gaze and was stunned at what she saw. Her wallet. At first she didn't believe her eyes, then in a flash, her worry fell away. She looked at Adam, joyful.

Without giving it a thought, she jumped at him, throwing her arms around his neck. His strong arms lifted her off her feet.

"Thank you, thank you," she said. She was hugging him right back. "Thank you!"

She inhaled his unique male scene and reveled in his strength and support, and for a moment, with her face nuzzling his neck, she let herself absorb the relief and the joy. Then she realized how close she was to a man she had no right to be so close to. Much less being lifted up and off her feet by him. The relief and joy were evaporating as quickly as they'd come, but the emotions flooding in to replace them were even more intense and unsettling.

ADAM HELD FAITH to him for as long as she'd let him, but then her mood shifted, the excitement of the wallet find faded, yet she was still clinging to him. He closed his eyes for a long moment, then slowly eased her down.

One look into her blue eyes told him that what was starting to stir in him wasn't one-sided. Her dark lashes swept low, partially hiding surprise and desire in the depths of her gaze. No, he wasn't alone in this at all.

On an impulse, he moved closer and dipped down to meet her lips with his. He deepened the connection and her arms drew him tightly to her.

He felt so tuned in to her at that moment, it stunned him, that and the undeniable fact that he could have stayed like that forever. Forever didn't seem like overkill to him at all. But forever turned out to be only as long as it took her to break the kiss and lightly push away from him.

He hesitated to let her go, not wanting whatever was happening to end. At the last moment, he framed her face with his hands and looked down into her eyes.

Her breathing was quick, her cheeks rosy-red. He exhaled unsteadily and said, "If this is how you show gratitude, I need to do something like this for you as often as I can." It was a feeble attempt at humor to try to cope with his feelings, but it didn't work.

There was no smile, no teasing between them, just Faith moving back to remove all contact with him. Her eyes darted to his hands, then past him. "My wallet?" she gasped.

His hands were empty, and for a moment he couldn't think what had happened to the wallet. Then he remembered tossing it onto the truck step when she'd all but leaped into his arms. Turning, he retrieved it and handed it to her, the worn leather damp from snow that was starting to fall again.

He watched her take it, but she didn't open it. She just stood there, and he thought for a moment that she was going to bail on dinner, but he wouldn't let her. "Do you want to walk or ride?"

His hunch proved right when she answered, "I don't think I'm going. I'm so tired," she said without meeting his gaze. "I'm sorry, so sorry." She sprinted away and up the porch steps. He stopped her just as she stepped into the reception area, and almost ran into her back when she stopped abruptly.

Mallory was there at the desk talking to Willie G., and both looked when the chime sounded. Mallory grinned at Faith and then at Adam behind her. "Hey, Adam, how's your dad doing?"

He closed the door behind him while Faith moved closer to the stairs. "When I left the hospital, my mother was with him, and Moses is convinced that it was an anxiety attack, not a heart attack."

"Your father's in the hospital?" Faith asked. "You never even mentioned it when we…when you took me there."

"It happened today. And my guess is he'll be out fairly soon."

"Thank goodness," Mallory said, and then she her spotted the wallet clutched in Faith's hands. "Oh, my gosh, you found it!"

Faith looked down at her wallet. "Yes, Adam found it in his truck."

"Well, good for you," Mallory said to

Adam. "Those special cop skills come in handy, don't they?"

"It fell out on my foot," he said. "It was caught between the door and the seat, I guess."

"Now you really do have another reason to celebrate, don't you?" she said to Faith.

Faith looked at her blankly. "Excuse me?"

"It's your birthday. Time to celebrate it!"

Adam saw Faith blanch at Mallory's words. "How did you know?" she asked.

"Your driver's license." Mallory motioned to the old-fashioned ledger on the desk where guests signed in. "I put down the number when you registered, and I saw your birth date on it." She tapped her head. "I have a photographic memory," she told them and then went on to reel off an address in Illinois. She looked at Faith inquiringly when she finished. "Did I get your address right?"

"Yes," Faith said, but Adam saw how she pressed a hand to her stomach during the exchange.

He didn't have a photographic memory, but he could certainly retain an address for a few hours. He'd remember it until he got back to the truck to write it down. He felt as if he were betraying her in some way, by checking on her, yet she didn't trust him. A kiss was born out of happiness, a spontaneous action. But trust was earned. He wished she'd trust him enough to tell him what was going on, but he honestly didn't think that he had enough time before she left town to earn her trust.

"Listen, I was going out, but that's just been canceled, and Willie G. came over to help and now he doesn't need to, so I ordered dinner from Casa Rosado Restaurant, and there is plenty coming. Why don't you both join us, and we can sing 'Happy Birthday' to Faith?"

Adam could see Faith figuring out how to get out of it, but he wouldn't let her. "She's hungry," he said without looking at her as he spoke. "She needs some food, and that would be perfect, not having to go out tonight when she's been so sick. Besides, it's snowing again."

Mallory clasped her hands together. "Wonderful." She looked right at Adam. "Plenty for you, too," she said. "And it's closer to the hospital than the ranch, just in case you're needed there."

He didn't hesitate. "Thanks. I'd like that." He looked at Faith, keeping his expression as unreadable as possible. "Casa Rosado has the best Mexican food in the area."

She still looked a little like a trapped animal, but she finally agreed, "It sounds good."

The front door opened and a kid came inside carrying a large cardboard box. Mallory came around the desk to go to the boy. "That was fast, Miguel." She inhaled exaggeratedly. "And it smells wonderful."

Adam moved over to the two of them and took the box out of the boy's hands while Mallory paid for the food. Willie G. motioned to him to follow him through the swinging doors and into the private area. Ten minutes later, the four of them were sitting around a large, well-used wooden table set by a bay window that overlooked the garden shrouded in snow.

The food was laid out, and there was little talk until the plates were full and the first tastes of the food were out of the way. Adam was across from Faith, watching her test the enchiladas and rice, then start to eat with a purpose. He smiled a bit, bent to eat, but not before he caught Mallory watching him. She lifted an eyebrow, smiled knowingly at him, then concentrated on her own plate.

Willie G. was silent for a long time, just eating methodically, and eventually he sat back. “I have to put this stuff on our menu,” he muttered. Then he shook his head, making his white braid bounce a little. “Nah, I’m no good at exotic foods.”

Adam laughed. “Since when are enchiladas and rice exotic?”

The chime sounded, and Willie G. jumped up without answering Adam. “I’ll get it. I came all this distance—I may as well do something besides eat.”

He went out, and was back, followed by Moses. The doctor stopped when he saw who was at the table, then crossed to Mallory. “I’m sorry about tonight. I thought I’d come by and see if we could get out for a quick bite, before I head back.” He motioned to the feast set out on the table. “Seems I’m late.”

Mallory got up and found another chair. Faith moved her chair and Moses took a seat at the table. “We have tons of ‘exotic’ food,” Mallory said, glancing at Willie G., who was digging into his meal again. “Please, have some with us. Besides, this is Faith's birthday."

Moses settled, took the plate Mallory passed to him and began to help himself to the food. "Your birthday?" he asked Faith.

"Yes, they tend to come once a year whether you want them to or not."

Adam laughed with the others, and he felt something settle in him. This had turned out better than he'd thought when he'd asked her to eat with him this evening. This was easier, less pressure, and Faith actually seemed to be relaxing as she ate.

Mallory apologized for her lack of drinks, offering milk, ice water, orange juice or lemon-lime soda. But Willie mixed the orange juice with the soda and made a drink that went well with the spicy food. They toasted to Faith's birthday.

FAITH SIPPED THE REFRESHING DRINK and glanced out the window at the garden, the same view she had from her room. She watched the snow falling steadily. She had wanted to go to dinner with Adam, and then after the kiss knew she couldn't. There was no way she could be in that truck again, not after her reaction to Adam kissing her. She'd liked it too much. She couldn't even look at him without reliving that moment. But being here in Mallory's kitchen with these folks was, for lack of a better description, nice and safe.

She wasn't alone in her room, and she wasn't alone with Adam. But he was there, grinning at the jokes Willie G. kept coming up with, looking relieved when Moses told him his father could go home tomorrow. Adam kept glancing at her with those dark eyes, sparking a heat in her that made her look away from him and concentrate on the others.

She hadn't expected this birthday to be anything but ignored, and here she was eating Mexican food, actually laughing and having the best time she'd experienced in months. She looked down at her plate as she put her glass back and was a bit surprised to see the food was almost gone. She'd been starving. She noted Moses and Mallory, not missing the constant contact between the two of them. A touch on the arm, a soft slap on the shoulder when Moses told the worst joke ever and the looks they gave each other.

"The most snow we've had around this

time of year, more than all the snow that's fallen in the past five years together." Willie G. was shaking his head. "Darnedest thing I've ever seen around here." He looked over at Faith. "I guess coming from Illinois, you're used to a lot more snow than this."

Faith nodded. "There was one year that I actually went out a second-story window and slid down to the backyard terrace." She knew she was talking too much, but the memory had always made her smile, especially the part when she landed in the deepest snow-drift she'd ever seen. "I finally figured out that sliding into a new snow drift wasn't a good idea."

She glanced at Adam, who was watching her intently. "Did you get in it and have to swim out?" he asked.

How could he know that? "Yes, and I thought I was a goner, but my dad grabbed me and pulled me out." That made her throat tighten, and she pushed her plate away. "That was wonderful. Thanks so much, Mallory."

"We aren't finished." The woman got up and went into a smaller room that looked as if it was lined with shelves of canned goods and bottles, probably a pantry. "I will be right there," her voice called out. "I just have to see if… Found it!" She sounded excited. "Now," she said as she appeared in the doorway with a small plate in her hand, "I just need something to light the candle."

Faith saw a cupcake on the plate as Mallory got closer, and the tightness in her throat translated to the threat of tears behind her eyes. She quickly took a breath and watched Mallory set a single chocolate cupcake in front of her. An oversize white candle stuck out of the thick chocolate frosting. Willie got up, leaned over the table and flipped open a cigarette lighter to touch it to the wick in the candle.

"Willie!" Mallory admonished, but he just stood back and flipped the lighter closed. "I gave up smoking going on fourteen years, but I never gave up carrying this thing." He held up the lighter fashioned in an intricate silver pattern with a single turquoise stone on one side. "The Council gave this to me, and it ain't going nowhere." He dropped it back into his shirt pocket and nodded at Faith. "Okay, young lady, make a wish, but just be careful about what you wish for, because any candle lit by my lighter guarantees that the wish will come true."

Faith looked at the dancing flame as Mallory led a rendition of "Happy Birthday to You," and when they finished, a wish popped into her head. She wanted *this* to be her reality, in this place with these people. But even as she blew the candle out, she knew that this would be the one wish that Willie G.'s lighter could not make come true.

The meal was over, and Faith knew it was time for reality to intrude. "I'm getting tired," she admitted. "Is it okay to take this up with me?"

"Of course it is," Mallory said.

Adam was staring at her, his eyes narrowed, but she couldn't look at him when he spoke. "I'm just sorry I didn't know it was your birthday, or you would have had some gifts."

She grabbed her wallet. "I have the best gift getting this back," she said, but knew that the only gift she needed, they'd given her without even knowing it—their time and company, not to mention their kindness. And Adam had given her something she'd treasure forever, long after she left this town to go back to her world. She picked up the plate and stood at the same time Adam got up and said he'd better be heading back to the ranch.

Mallory looked at Adam. "You know, the snow's coming down pretty hard, and I was thinking you shouldn't be driving out to the ranch in it. Besides, if your mother needs you, you might not be able to make it back." Faith watched Adam's expression show concern. "Not that I think you'll be needed, but why don't you stay here? It's one less thing to worry about."

He paused first, but then said, "Do you have a room available?"

"The other one on the top floor is empty until tomorrow, so it's perfect." Mallory smiled. "And you can carry Faith's jacket and cupcake up for her."

Moses said, "I need to get going, too." Then he stopped as if he remembered something. "Oh, Adam, I meant to tell you that Jack called when I was leaving."

"Why did he call you?"

Moses almost smiled at that. "Hey, don't kill the messenger. He said your phone was going directly to voice mail."

That seemed to mollify him. "What did he call for?"

"Your mom left a message about your dad and he wanted to find out what was going on."

Adam nodded, obviously satisfied with that explanation. "Anything else?"

Moses shook his head. "No, he just said to keep him in the loop. Oh, and he wished me a merry Christmas."

Adam's face tightened. "Great."

Moses held up a hand again. "Adam, this is all good. The man's doing something to move on after Robyn's death, and we need to encourage him. He can't stay stuck in the past forever. He's got to live his life, to figure it out."

Faith thought she might be the only one to see Mallory's expression soften, then turn to something bordering on pain. The words had struck her hard, and Faith knew that coming from Moses, they struck even deeper. She knew that the man cared about her, and she thought Mallory was coming close to falling for him, to moving on from her past. Moses turned to Mallory, speaking softly. "I'm sorry," he said. "I wasn't thinking and—"

"Moses, Moses," Willie G. said as he rocked back in his chair to look up at the others all standing around the table now. "You didn't say nothing wrong, and Mallory knows that you didn't mean a thing by anything you said." He glanced at his niece, almost daring her to argue with him. "Don't you, Mal?"

She managed a slight smile for Moses. "He's right. Willie G.'s always right," she said, reaching to close the food containers.

Faith felt like a third wheel and said, "Good night, and thanks again." She started to go upstairs.

"Good sleeping," Willie G. called after her. To Adam he said, "Tell your dad I'm here if he needs anything."

"Sure will," Adam said and grabbed the jackets. Faith already had the cupcake plate and her wallet with her.

Faith was very aware of Adam following her up the stairs and the fact that he was going to stay in the room next door for the night. She got to her room, managed to open the door, then stepped in to put the cupcake on the desk and toss her wallet onto the bed. When she faced Adam, he had put her jacket on the chair over her purse, and he stood silhouetted in the doorway, backlit by the soft lights in the hallway.

She was awed by the sight of him and thinking of how honorable a man he was. She managed to say "Thanks" as she crossed to where he stood. "I enjoyed tonight."

"I did, too. Very much."

She hoped she wasn't blushing like a teenager, because she felt like one, remembering their kiss. "I hope your dad's going to be okay."

"He will be," Adam said, then he lifted a hand to tenderly stroke her cheek. "Happy birthday, Faith," he breathed, then bent and brushed her lips with his.

The contact was as light as the tickle of a feather, but it made it impossible for her to do anything but stand there. "Sleep well," he murmured, tapping her chin with his forefinger. He smiled, turned and left the room.

She quickly closed the door and collapsed on the bed. Today had been a short day, with her sleeping until after three o'clock, but it had definitely been one of the best, filled with things she'd never thought possible. She'd found her wallet, been kissed, had an impromptu birthday party with new friends, made a crazy wish, then been kissed again. Crazy.

She got up from the bed, undressed, then picked up the cupcake. Nibbling at the chocolate frosting, she held up the single candle in front of her. "Happy birthday to me," she whispered and thought this was as close to happy as she was going to feel for a very long time. She knew it wouldn't last, but she'd embrace it and not let it go until she had no choice in the matter.

CHAPTER THIRTEEN

ADAM TOSSED HIS JACKET and hat on the neatly made bed before he pulled out his cell phone from his pocket. He frowned at the blank screen, then grabbed his jacket again, put it on and quietly opened his door.

He walked carefully along the hall, seeing a ribbon of light at the bottom of Faith's door, then turned and went downstairs. He found Willie G. by the fireplace all settled in an overstuffed chair, and from the sounds of snoring coming from him, he assumed the old guy was asleep. There were hushed voices in the kitchen, and he was ready to just walk out without saying anything. But the swinging door flew back and Moses was there.

He stopped when he saw Adam, then came around the desk. "Have to go. Got an emergency." Adam must have made a face because his friend touched his arm. "Not Herbert. He's doing just fine."

As Moses got to the door, Adam caught up with him and said, "Tell Mom I'm over here if she needs me. I've got to find my phone charger and get my phone up and working again."

"Sure thing," Moses said, hurrying out, heading for his sedan parked next to Adam's truck. The doctor was gone before Adam made it to his truck and got in. He opened the glove compartment, found the charger, plugged it in and connected the dead phone. As soon as he started the motor, the LED screen on the phone lit up with an animated battery that indicated it was being charged.

He reached across to take out a scrap of paper and a pen, then he quickly wrote down the address in Rockford, Illinois, that Mallory had recited earlier. He glanced at the dash clock. Just after ten. He needed to do something before going back into the inn.

Adam backed out and onto the street. He turned in the direction of the police station and hoped that John had the late shift. When he got there and went inside, a deputy named Nate was manning the front desk.

The guy shot Adam a glance. "Sir, can I help you?"

"Looking for the chief."

"He's got the night off, but he just came in saying he'd left something in his office."

Adam nodded his thanks. John was standing behind his desk, pulling on his uniform jacket over his street clothes when he looked up at Adam. "Just going to call you to ask about your dad."

"Dad's okay. He's going home tomorrow. Moses thinks it was nothing more than an anxiety attack."

"That's good to hear. What about the dinner tomorrow night? Your mom won't be in any shape to have most of her family over, will she? And Hannah says she's feeling a cold coming on."

"Don't underestimate Mom. She'll have it, but I know she'll understand if you two can't make it."

"Give your folks our love and wish them merry Christmas from us. Now I have to fix up Santa's mistake. He forgot one of the most important toys for a kid named Cody, otherwise known as my son. The chief of police needs to pick up the pieces once again."

"I need to pick up some pieces, too," Adam said. "And I need your computer to do it."

"I won't ask. I don't have time to untangle your reasoning, but—" John swept a hand in the direction of his desk "—make yourself comfortable. Just log out when you're done."

"You got it." Adam took a seat at the desk. John went to the door and turned at the last minute. "This is about that lady, isn't it?"

Adam nodded. "Yes."

"Good luck," he said and pulled the door shut behind him.

Adam settled behind the computer, not bothering to do more than unbutton his jacket. Then he took out the scrap of paper with the address on it. He copied it into the search field and hit Enter. It only took a few seconds for it to come back as a valid address, but it was owned by a Jesse & Son's Investments. He did a search on that and found the company had been started by a law firm in the Chicago area, and the name connected to it was Baron Little, a top attorney in that city. That told him nothing about Faith.

He knew he was doing something wrong and suddenly the solution came to him. It wasn't the address that was the key; it was the birth date. He went into the special-search area that was unlocked by John's second password, 3CCCboys, standing for John's three sons, Cody, Cash and Clay. The screen blossomed on the monitor and he put in Faith's birth date.

He knew that most people kept a first name or something close to it but often changed their last name. Oddly, they usually used the same initial of their surname for their fake name. He decided on simply Faith A., but got nothing. Then he started through the alphabet and when he got to *S* he hit pay dirt.

The list gave full names and less-used versions of the main name in the results. Faith Marie Sizemore, then Faith Sizemore, followed by Marie Sizemore and Faith M. Sizemore. He stared at the list, but none of them were associated with the address in Rockford. Either he'd turned up a result with the same first two names or the Faith he knew was really Faith Marie Sizemore from Chicago.

The birth certificate that came up validated that he'd found Faith. The name on the certificate was Faith Marie Sizemore, father Raymond Allan Sizemore, mother Gabriella Marie Arden. “Arden,” he breathed as he stared at the screen. He put in a search for Faith Marie Sizemore and watched a huge amount of matches come up on the screen.

After sifting through the results, he knew who Faith Marie Sizemore was and why she was hiding out in Wolf Lake, New Mexico, trying her hardest to stay away from people. Her mixed reactions to mentions of her father made complete sense, and her fear of John, of cops, made even more sense. The last article said that the government had been expected to subpoena her for the grand jury being convened with respect to possible indictments against her father and various other officers of the corporation. But they had had to continue without her testimony because she had disappeared.

He raked his fingers through his hair and let out a hissing breath. She had to be scared to death. From what little he knew about her, he could feel the strength of her attachment to her father. One story told about her mother dying when Faith was very young, and no siblings were ever mentioned. The idea of forcing her to testify against her own father turned Adam's stomach, no matter what the father had done.

A picture of Faith was part of the results, and she looked lovely. Her hair had been longer, pulled sleekly back from her delicate face with no curls showing, but the style emphasized her eyes. The look there was heartbreaking for Adam. Scared to death and trying to act as if she was in control.

He sat up, reached for the computer and hit a few buttons to get to the browsing history. He emptied the cache, then exited every screen he had opened. The last page he had left on the screen was the picture. He knew what he should do and he knew what he would do. They were diametrically opposite to each other. He wanted Faith to trust him, to tell him what was going on. He wanted that with every fiber of his being.

He logged off, rebuttoned his jacket and headed out. He said good-night to the deputy, then stepped out into falling snow. It was still coming down, blanketing everything in white. A slight parting in the heavy clouds let out a glimmer of moonlight to dance on the crystals of snow, before more clouds came and it disappeared.

Adam got into the truck, looked at his phone, saw the charge was complete and there had been no calls. He slipped it into his jacket pocket and headed for the hospital. He found a nurse who took him up to the fourth floor and his father's room. Looking in the door, he saw his mother on a cot butted up against the hospital bed, inches from his father. They were both sleeping peacefully, her right and his left hand holding on to each other. He backed out without waking them.

With the nurse promising to contact him if there was any change, Adam headed back to the inn. He stepped into total silence, ruined only by the chime when the door opened. Mallory didn't appear, and the chair where Willie G. had been sleeping was empty. It was almost midnight when he went up the stairs, paused as he looked down the hallway to Faith's room. There was no light under the door now. Turning, he went to his room, got ready for bed quickly, then lay down.

Faith Sizemore. He never would have found out who she was if he hadn't thought about the birth-date angle. For a moment, he wished he hadn't gotten so lucky. No, he wished that Faith had told him. When her car was ready, he knew she would be gone, so if he had a wish right then, it would be for Dent to take more time fixing the car. That would keep her here, keep her close and give him time to figure out how to reach her.

When he'd almost kissed her the first time, he'd felt that chink in his honor and thought it had been a single slip. He'd prided himself on his work, on taking no shortcuts or playing fast and loose to get what he wanted. His personal life was no different. He'd stopped that kiss because of the feeling of being self-serving. Now he was holding information he knew would help the prosecution's case in the Raymond Sizemore trial, if there was a trial, but the cost of turning her over to them was too great.

He had to have a plan, figure out how to save Faith while still doing his job. He knew then that the night would be long. And it was.

FAITH WOKE TO LIGHT cutting through the small opening in the curtains. She'd doubted she would sleep well, but she had, with wispy dreams that came and went, and she felt rested when she sat up and rubbed her eyes. She sat there for a long moment, then reached for the cell phone on the nightstand and put in her father's number.

The phone rang once, twice, before it was picked up. "Dad?" she said cautiously.

"Yes." She heard the relief in his tone.

"I just want you to know that I'm okay."

"It was your birthday," he said with obvious pain.

"Yes, and I'll have more." She closed her eyes. "I just wanted to let you know I'm fine and that I won't call for a while. I know what's going on there."

"Is something wrong on your end?"

She looked at the clock. They'd been speaking for twenty seconds. She'd given herself a limit of thirty seconds. "No, no, I have to go. I love you," she said quickly and hung up.

She sank back, and the next time she looked at the time, it was nine o'clock. She got out of bed and dressed in a turtleneck and jeans. Pushing on her boots, she grabbed her jacket and wallet and stepped out of her room. As she turned to the stairs, she stopped.

Adam was coming out of his room, followed by a woman bundled up in a calf-length coat. Before she could step back into the room, Adam looked up and saw her. "Faith," he called and came to her with the lady. He stopped, smiled at her and said, "Good morning," then he glanced at the woman with him. "Mom, this is Faith. Faith, my mother, Lark Carson. She came by to tell me about my father."

Adam's mother. She was lovely, with dark hair streaked with gray twisted into a low knot, and her skin was just like that of a much younger woman. She smiled at Faith as she held out her hand to her, and Faith knew where her son got his dimple. His mother had the same smile.

When Faith clasped her hand, Lark held hers in both of hers and spoke in a soft, almost singsong voice. "Nice to meet you. I saw you at our party, but I didn't have a chance to say hello to you then. I hear there is a belated happy birthday in order."

"Oh, thank you," Faith said as she drew her hand back. "Nice to meet you. Is everything okay with your husband?"

"He's doing very well, thank you. Adam told me you're here all alone, that your car isn't working, so you're pretty much stuck in Wolf Lake for now."

Adam had summed that up pretty well, she thought. "I hope to have my car going pretty soon, probably today or tomorrow at the latest."

"Good, good, Dent is a good boy and he'll make it right." She turned to Adam. "I have an idea," she said and she looked back at Faith. "Since you're stuck here, why not come to our dinner this evening? We're having some friends, and we would love to have you join us." Before Faith could refuse without offending the lady, Lark patted Adam's arm and said, "You tell her about it, and you can drive her." She smiled warmly at Faith. "We will be expecting you. Dinner's served at eight."

Then Lark leaned up to kiss Adam on the cheek and waved at Faith as she started down the stairs. "And make sure Adam drives carefully. He tends to think he's chasing the bad guys all the time, and goes too fast. See you there!"

Adam was grinning at her. "She won't take no for an answer," he said, and she knew he was right. He flicked his gaze over her. "Where are you off to?"

"Dent's. To check on my car."

"Good, I'll drop you there." Before she could say no, he added, "It's on my way to the hospital, and it's a cold walk to Dent's even when it isn't snowing."

She'd take the ride, she decided. As they started down the stairs, she asked, "Your father's really okay?"

"Mom wouldn't have come here if he wasn't," Adam said as they reached the bottom.

"They're devoted?" she asked, really wanting to know.

"They always have been, in both good and bad times. My mother's never faltered." She could hear a hint of pride in his tone.

"I think that's the way my parents were. But my mother passed away when I was so young, so I barely remember her."

Mallory was speaking to an older couple at the registration desk, looked up to see Faith and Adam, waved and continued with her guests. Faith stepped outside and was stunned by the snow-covered scene in front of her. About a foot of the white stuff had fallen during the night, and it was twice as deep in some spots due to the snow cleared from the road.

"A guaranteed white Christmas," Adam said as the door closed behind them. His breath fogged the frigid air, and the sun shining meant the icy snow glittered like diamonds.

"Beautiful," Faith agreed, the peace in this place almost tangible. Right then, she hated the thought of leaving, and when Adam touched her arm to lead her to the truck, she really hated it that she had no alternative but to turn her back on everything here.

They got into the truck and Adam drove slowly down the street still slick with the snow and ice. He picked up their conversation from the stairs. "You were pretty young when your mom died?"

"Yes, I barely remember her, or maybe I just think I remember her because my dad has never stopped talking about her."

Adam exhaled. "My brother Jack's like that. He married the love of his life, and when Robyn died, I thought Jack's life was over. He's had a hard time with his grief."

Faith fingered her wallet. "And you came back for him?"

"Yes, but to be totally honest, after years

of heading away from here, I think I needed to come back for me, as well."

"I felt that way when I went to college. I was so grateful to go home when I finished my degree."

"I thought about college for a hot second, but knew that I wanted to be a cop. I went through the academy, then eventually left for greener pastures. I told you I'm in Dallas now, but I'm thinking of making another change."

She looked around the town, wondering why he'd choose to leave this. "Wolf Lake wasn't where you wanted to be?"

"No, I didn't want to be here," he said, and she could have sworn he looked surprised to admit that. "I've always wanted to be someplace else. I mean, I love it here, I had a great childhood, but for some reason I wanted to see what was beyond all this."

"And now you've seen it?"

"Yes, I have." He drove in silence, stopping for a group of shoppers to make their way across the road, then he kept going.

"And?"

He glanced at her, then at the road. "And

I came back." He turned into Dent's parking area and stopped. "At least for now."

Faith noticed Dent by the gas pump, talking to a tall, lean man, who apparently owned a huge truck with mismatched fenders. When he spotted Adam's truck, Dent said goodbye to the other man and came over to them. He saw Faith in the cab and went to her side. As the window buzzed down, he grabbed the door frame and pulled himself up to lean into the cab to talk to her. "Good news, darling, your car's going to be done later on today."

Faith knew she should be thrilled, but for some reason it was hard for her to smile. "Thank you," she said.

He looked past her to Adam and then back. He added hastily, "At least, it should be. Tomorrow at the very latest," he said slowly. "Uh, tomorrow by day's end. Before Christmas. I'll call you at Mallory's when it's ready."

Faith wasn't sure what had just happened, but her car was going to be finished. That was all that should matter. "I really appreciate it. How much will I owe you?"

He glanced past her again. The figure he

named was half of what he'd estimated before. "Are you sure?" she asked.

"Yes, I had some parts here already. I forgot. And the labor cost the most. But it's all going to be fixed just fine. Should take you on your journey without any more trouble." He jumped back down and waved to her. "I'll call you."

The window went up, and Faith looked over at Adam. He shrugged. "I told you Dent could do it."

"Yes, you did," she said.

"Where are you going now?"

She grabbed the handle and opened the door. "I need to do a few things." Holding her wallet, she climbed out and turned to look back up at Adam. "Thank you," she said and meant it.

"Are you sure?"

"Yes." Although she wasn't sure what he was asking.

"Okay, I'll pick you up around seven for dinner."

She'd forgotten all about Lark's invitation. "I don't want to intrude, and your dad's been sick."

"Mom wants you there. Seven," he said.

She swung the door shut and stood back when Adam slowly drove off the lot and out onto the street. She watched the big black truck for only a moment before heading back the way she'd come with Adam. She stopped at the coffee shop, picked up a few things, then went straight to the inn to wait for Dent's call.

Once in her room, she glanced at the computer. After her last experience at the computer, she'd thought of not looking through the rest of the documents. She knew enough to know where she stood. Actually, the idea of another migraine coming was a good excuse to not go anywhere near the computer for now. She knew the real reason was the fear that she'd find more things that could be used against her dad.

She moved around the room, looked out the window at the garden covered in snow, then headed downstairs. Willie G. was there, sitting behind the desk, reading a book on learning French. "Hi," she said and he looked up.

"Hey, missy. How're you doing?"

"Well, I'm waiting for a call from Dent at the garage."

"Oh, yeah, that car of yours. Heard it's almost done."

He heard everything, she guessed. "That's the word." She glanced at his book. "You're learning French?"

He nodded. "A man can't get too educated, and after all, French is the language of love." He smiled slyly. "Never too old for that, huh?"

"I guess not," she agreed. "Could you let me know if Dent calls?"

"Sure, and when Mallory gets back, I'll pass it on to her."

"Where did she go?"

"I don't rightly know." He closed his book and laid it on the desk. Turning to put both elbows on the polished wood, he rested his chin in his hands. "She said she had to go out, and since I was staying until the roads are cleared south of town, she asked me to watch the place."

"I'll be in my room."

"I can call you when Adam comes to get you, if I'm still here."

She stared at him. He knew Adam would be coming to pick her up later on? "Where did you hear about that?"

"Let's see," he said, scrunching up his face in concentration as if trying to remember. "I saw Oscar when I went over to get Mallory some cream, and he said that he'd talked to Moses and he said that Mrs. Carson had mentioned to him that you were going to dinner at their place." He snapped his fingers. "And that's who said that Adam was going to drive you out to the ranch."

She laughed despite her circumstances. The man was a human gossip chain and she kind of liked that; it showed people cared. "Yes, call me down when Adam gets here."

He gave a little salute, picked up his French vocabulary book and said, "Au revoir, missy."

She nodded. "Very nice." When she was upstairs in her room again, she laughed some more. Nothing was private in Wolf Lake, she thought, not when you had a grapevine that covered just about every resident and visitor. Good thing there weren't any national-security secrets around here, and she laughed so hard her stomach started to hurt.

As the laughter subsided, she felt a sense of loss replace it. An almost staggering sense of loss. This would be but a memory tomorrow. Just a memory.

ADAM DROVE TO the hospital on the newly cleared roads and smiled about Dent. The man knew cars, but being subtle hadn't ever been his strong suit. Though he'd caught on pretty quickly when Adam had held up a hand that Faith couldn't see and mouthed *No* when he'd been ready to promise to have the car done today. He'd segued to tomorrow, and a thumbs-up from Adam urged him to tell her absolutely before Christmas. Adam had mimed holding a phone to his ear, and Dent had caught on right away, promising to call her when it was ready. Probably his scowl had stopped Dent from giving her a figure for the job that would have caused her to choke.

He pulled into the hospital parking lot and went inside to find out how soon his father would be released. As he walked through the doors, his cell phone rang and he pulled it out of his pocket. Dent. He answered it. "Hey, there."

"Yeah, and now tell me why you acted like that when you were here with the lady?"

"I just wanted her to be around a bit longer," he said.

"So you had to act it out. Why didn't you

just tell her you wanted her to stick around instead of making me lie to her?"

"Is her car done right now?"

"No, of course it isn't."

"Then you didn't lie."

"How does that work for you, rationalizing stuff like that when you're a cop?"

He cringed at the question, but knew that keeping Faith around a bit longer wasn't just to get her story from her. He didn't want her to leave for personal reasons. He cleared his throat, and it occurred to him that he was very close to maybe loving the woman. A woman who had lied to him from the start and had kept lying. "I'm not a cop right now," he said, a weak explanation at best.

"I'd say you weren't, brother."

"Agreed. I was just hoping you could drag this out until tomorrow. Don't call her until around four, okay?"

"Tomorrow's Christmas Eve. I don't plan on being here past two or so."

"Try for four."

"Okay, but I still think you should just tell her to stay put for a while."

He wished it was that easy, but suddenly nothing was easy about Faith or him. Now he really needed her to trust him, way beyond telling him her side of the story. "Thanks, I owe you," he said. "And I do owe you the rest of the bill."

"You do," he said and he hung up.

Adam put his phone away, then headed to the fourth floor. He'd take his dad home, get him settled, then head back to town to get Faith. He had his answers about Faith, and now he had to make a decision about what to do. He didn't want to be a cop and confront her. He just wanted her to trust him enough to tell him, and he had to make that happen before four in the afternoon the next day.

CHAPTER FOURTEEN

FAITH HAD HOPED for a reprieve from going to the Carson family dinner, but none came. Dent had called, but only to tell her that the car wouldn't be done until the next day and probably not until around four o'clock. Part of her wanted to be with Adam again, but being with him was just plain dangerous and would end up being painful. He touched her on some level that she couldn't explain and wouldn't explore. The less she understood about her reactions to the man, the better off she'd be.

Right at seven o'clock, she heard the chime ring downstairs and took one last look at herself. Her red blouse and the dark pants she'd worn to the dance were the closest things she had with her that could be considered dressy. She slipped on her simple black flats. She almost longed for heels, anything to minimize the way Adam towered over her.

Her makeup was just lipstick and a touch of eye shadow. Her curls were their own master, and she would have loved to have had her long hair again, to tame it into a low chignon.

She leaned closer to the mirror; looking into her own eyes, she could see the uneasiness about going to this dinner. Adam's parents. Friends of the family. She had no right being there at all. She paced the room until she heard muffled voices below.

Quickly, she grabbed her purse, pushed her wallet into it, then picked up her jacket and put it on. She'd wait there until Mallory came up to tell her Adam had arrived. By the time there was a knock on her door, she was more than ready to get it over with. But when she opened the door and found Adam standing there instead of Mallory, she was hit by a truth that she'd pushed away one too many times. And now it was there with a vengeance.

Adam Carson only had to show up to become the center of her world. She barely fought back a gasp as she acknowledged the thought and knew it would never go away again.

Adam ran his gaze over her with excruciating slowness, and by the time his eyes met hers, she could almost taste the tension. The center of her world? He was very close to being her world. But what a world she had. Certainly not one that he'd ever want to share with her. "Ready to go?" he asked.

She wanted to hold on to him and never let him go. "Ready," she managed.

He stood back and she went out, pulling the door shut behind her, then she hurried to the stairs, keeping ahead of him until they got to the front door in the deserted reception area. Adam came up behind her, then reached past her to grab the handle and pull the door back. She ducked past, trying to ignore the scent of aftershave and maleness as she headed for the truck.

As they drove away from the inn, Adam spoke, and when he did, his question confused Faith. "So does it bother you that I'm with the police?"

This was not a good way to start the evening. "Everyone has a job, at least, most do."

"You know what the motto is of most police forces, don't you?"

"What?" She had no idea where this was going. A rising fear was growing inside her. She should have refused to do this and remained at the inn. She was only one day away from making her escape.

"Protect and Serve. It's a standard. Some have others, such as in London, it's Fidelity, Bravery and Integrity. In Scotland, it's Semper Vigilo, translated, Always Vigilant, but here, as I said, it's Protect and Serve."

She still didn't get it. "What does that have to do with anything?"

"I just wanted you to know," he said.

"That's it?" she asked.

"Yes, what did you expect?"

"I don't know, maybe another Willie G. joke."

He chuckled at that. As they neared the outskirts of town, the road narrowed to only being wide enough to allow for two lanes given snow piled high on both sides. "I've missed Willie G. and his horrible jokes. I think I've missed a lot in the past few years."

"Being in Dallas has to be a lot different than being here."

"It is." His expression seemed unreadable to her. "Lately, I've been thinking of making some changes in my life."

"Isn't that what life's all about, changes?"

"You sound as if you know all about changes," he said, his focus still on the road.

Her life had turned upside down. "Doesn't everyone?"

"Some more than others."

Faith felt a tug at her heart. She'd once thought the most jarring change in her life had come when the federal agents stormed the firm's offices. Yet she realized that a big change in her life had occurred when she'd run into Adam the first night she was in Wolf Lake. And another one was coming tomorrow.

"Everyone I know seems to be going through some sort of change in their lives, some minor, some very major," he said.

She heard him exhale, and instead of looking over at him, she turned to the side window and the night outside.

He continued, "Jack and Mallory have endured huge changes and their lives will never be the same."

She was uneasy with the conversation. She

didn't want to think about the way lives were altered forever in a second. She was living through that horror. Her hands were aching where they clutched at her purse, and she forced her fingers to loosen. "We don't have choices in things like that," she said softly.

"True, but I still wish Jack would talk to me about what's happening with him. He's so closed and handling it on his own. That's no good for anyone."

"It's the way he has to deal with things," she said, knowing she had no choice about her actions. She'd had to leave, to keep moving and stay low. She'd never dreamed she'd end up in a truck in a small town with a cop and not be under arrest.

That last thought made her want to laugh and scream; she wasn't sure which one was the right reaction. "Everyone has to do what they have to do."

"Can I write that down?" he asked, a tinge of humor coloring his words, and miraculously, she almost smiled.

"Be my guest," she said, wanting to change the conversation, to forget about the past and tomorrow. Tonight was all there was, and she found that she desperately wanted it that way. "You know, I never got to see the lake."

"What?"

"Wolf Lake. I never got to see the lake that the town was named after."

For some reason, that made Adam chuckle. "I'm not sure how to put this, but there is no lake. Not a lake anywhere around here."

"But someone said that I needed to go see the lake. I remember that, I think."

"You're right. I'm sure someone suggested you should visit the lake. It's just the word *lake* isn't exactly right."

She turned to him as he spoke and she didn't miss the touch of humor playing at the corners of his lips. "What word would be exactly right?"

"Hmm, if you get on a horse and ride toward the high country where my mother's people first settled, you'll go past a formation that was probably carved out by water aeons ago. It's a half circle, bowl-like on a high plateau, with a jutting ledge that overlooks everything below. The half circle, maybe a half a mile across, has some good soil and a certain grass grows there in the spring. It's thick and tall, and it's got this odd shimmering effect to it."

He slowed and she glanced ahead. The glow in the distance changed into lit iron lanterns sitting on heavy stone posts. "How does that get called a lake?"

He slowed more as he spoke. "When there's a perfect full moon and a breeze kicking up at night, the grass moves with the wind. It looks just like a body of water with waves rippling across it."

"That's Wolf Lake?"

"It is, but I suspect the name Wolf Lake came from a wish that there was a lake somewhere nearby. It certainly sounded better than Wolf Desert, or Wolf Barrens, or even Wolfville."

Adam steered the truck through the entrance to the ranch, the same route she and Mallory had taken when they'd come for the party. But this time they turned away from the huge barn and went up a small rise to the main house. The two-story adobe hacienda sat in the night, lights blazing on both floors and about a dozen cars and trucks parked at a circle at the top of a cobbled driveway.

Holly and berries were strung around the

porch and over the door, and when Adam pushed on the carved wooden barrier, laughter and music splashed out into the night. The main room went from the front of the house to the back wall that was all windows, except for an impressive stone fireplace in the middle.

Heavy leather furniture decorated the space. The ceiling soared above two stories. Christmas details dominated, from a tree standing in the raised entry where they stepped inside, with gifts piled under it, to garlands along the staircase railing. There were a lot of people, everyone in animated conversations.

"Merry, merry Christmas," Adam's mother called to them as she broke away from two couples near the fireplace. She was dressed in a pretty green velvet dress that set off her skin and eyes. She hugged Adam, then turned to Faith, who expected a handshake at the most, but found herself being hugged, too.

Lark stood back, looking from one to the other, and motioned to the party behind her. "Have a bit to eat, but not too much because dinner will be ready soon."

"Whcre's Dad?" Adam asked.

"Upstairs lying down for a minute. He might come down for dinner, but I told him he didn't have to."

"He's okay?"

"Yes, except for Moses telling him what he can or can't do for a while." She smiled at Faith. "Herbert is so stubborn."

Faith didn't know what to say, so she just nodded, hoping it was okay to agree with her. "Thank you for inviting me," she said.

"Oh, dear, I should thank you for coming." She patted Faith on the arm. "I'll send R.J. over for your jackets," she said, and with that she was heading across the room toward a man carrying a tray of drinks. He came over to Faith and Adam.

"Your jackets?" he asked, his hand extended.

"How did she talk you into this?" Adam asked, shrugging out of his leather coat, handing it to him.

R.J. was as tall as Adam, probably around twenty or so and never stopped smiling. "Honestly, money. Your parents are very generous with the help." He turned to take

Faith's jacket. "Have a great time," he said and disappeared.

"R.J.'s Dent's nephew," he explained to Faith.

"The guests are family friends?" she asked, looking over the party of women in casual clothes and men mostly in jeans and loose shirts. Every one of the men seemed to be wearing cowboy boots.

"Mostly family," Adam said, and for the next half hour or so, he hugged the ladies and shook hands with the men, all the time explaining to Faith who everyone was and how they were all connected.

She met aunts and uncles, godfathers, cousins, second cousins and plenty of folks to whom he referred to as "our people." He meant the Wolf family—some were from the reservation, others from town and still others from farther away. She was overwhelmed, but Adam didn't miss a beat. And by the time dinner was announced, she couldn't remember who was who or how they were related. Thank goodness no one gave her a test. She would have failed miserably.

The dining room was large enough to hold a massive table that, from her calculations, held twenty-eight people for dinner, plus the two of them to make thirty. Lark sat at the foot of the table, but the chair at the head of the table was empty when Adam's father didn't come down for the meal.

Jack was still gone, and Adam's younger brother, Gage, wasn't there, either. "I never know where he is," Adam told her as the first course was being served. "Gage travels all over for business. Last I heard he couldn't even think of coming home until next month."

"Adam," Lark said, raising her voice for her son to hear her. "Gage will be here when he can be, and Jack will be, too."

Her tone was firm and Adam didn't argue. As they ate, Adam explained the food to Faith. The meal was a traditional one in the Wolf family. There were favorites of the boys—the tamales, the corn bread, a salsa that held more heat in a drop than most hot sauces did in a bottle. Faith's eyes watered and Adam gave her a plain flour tortilla to eat to absorb most of the heat. The main course was "Our version of pheasant," Adam explained. But she still didn't know what it was called, because the name he gave it had no translation from their native tongue to English.

By the time dessert was serve—a small jar of honey provided to each diner and chunks of what looked like pound cake drizzled with a berry sauce—Faith had stopped asking for labels. She just enjoyed it, and if she couldn't pronounce the names, she was okay with that.

When they adjourned to the living room again, Faith sat by Adam on a deep comfortable couch. She fought the urge to just lean into him and relax. She gazed around the room, at people who meant a lot to each other, an extended family that gave new meaning to the word *extended,* and she felt sad that both she and Adam had walked away from family. They had to be fools.

Lark stood up and got everyone's attention. "Present time," she declared and motioned to a couple of guests to help her. One by one gifts were taken from under the tree and given to each guest, accompanied by a kiss from Lark. The distribution was done so each person eventually had a gift in their lap, then Lark turned, motioned Adam to the tree. He got up, removed an ornament off a middle branch, then went to give it to his mother. He handed her what looked like a small blue foil box, then Lark crossed to Faith and handed it to her. “Merry Christmas,” the woman said softly, stooped and kissed Faith on the cheek. She then smiled, her arms outstretched to the room. “Everyone open your present.”

Faith stared at the small box in her palm, and Adam settled back by her. She met his gaze, hoping he couldn’t see the tears that were starting to form. “What is this?” she asked, hearing the tightness in her own voice.

“Open it,” he said softly, and his arm went around her shoulders. She undid the ribbon on the box with unsteady fingers, murmuring, “I didn’t get anyone anything.”

“You came. That’s present enough,” Adam said close to her ear, and the threat of tears increased.

She wished he wasn’t so close or so kind, and she wished she had never come. Wrong was wrong, and she’d really been wrong. Refusing the invitation would have been better than sitting here close to crying, wishing she could burrow into Adam’s hold and never leave.

Lark came to sit down by Faith. "Open it," she urged gently.

Faith hesitated, then lifted the lid and found a smaller, hand-carved, circular box. She took it out and lifted the top to find a small, polished turquoise stone in the shape of a teardrop lying on a bed of white velvet.

"It's a memory stone," Lark said as she reached to pluck it out of the box and hold it up for Faith to see. "It stores up only good memories, and when things are hard or stressful," she told Faith as she closed Faith's fingers around the stone, "you can hold on to it and remember the best of times."

Faith wanted so dearly to believe this—that she really could store up good memories for when she was alone and scared. When she needed someone the likes of whom she'd never see again.

Adam laid his hand over hers, his fingers closing on hers, warm and gentle. "My grandfather, Jackson Wolf, found these stones when he was clearing the land years ago to build the original adobe north of here. He found enough for each child and each grandchild as they came along."

Faith looked at him. "I can't take this."

"Of course you can. He made them for friends, too." He squeezed her hand reassuringly. "He polished them and made the boxes, as well." He let go of her and reached for the open neck of his shirt. He pushed his forefinger under his collar, then pulled back and he'd hooked a silver chain with a stone identical to the one she was holding. "I got mine when I was ten. The old man gave them when folks needed them, not at any set time or age." He tucked it back under his shirt. "Mom wants you to have that, so you must need it."

Faith exhaled, quickly put the stone back into the box and held on to it tightly. "Thank you so much," she said to Lark in a voice that wasn't entirely steady. She stood. "I'm sorry, but I really need to get back."

Adam said nothing, and Lark simply gave her a hug and stepped back. "You are welcome here whenever you are in Wolf Lake."

"Thank you," she said, and R.J. was there with her jacket.

Adam held the jacket for her, then as she put it on, he lightly smoothed her shoulders. She picked up her purse but kept the box in her free hand.

Once in the truck, Faith sat very still, feeling the pressure of her grip on the box as they headed back to the inn. Adam glanced at her but didn't speak until the ranch was behind them in the darkness. "Are you okay?"

"Yes, I'm fine, but I feel badly that I didn't have anything for your mother." That was true, but so insignificant compared to what was going on inside her at that point.

"Believe me, she didn't expect anything."

What Faith thought of as an evening to get through had turned out to be so overwhelming that she could barely absorb it. "Thank you for taking me," she said. Memories for the stone, she thought. Already she was storing them up for a future so uncertain that it frightened her.

His hand unexpectedly reached out to cover hers holding the box. "You're upset," he said, not a question, but a statement.

"I'm just… I didn't expect anything like the party. I thought it was dinner, but your family, goodness, they were everywhere, and your mother was terrific, even though your dad's been so sick. And I shouldn't have gone."

"Why?"

The single word froze her in place. Everything in her wanted to just tell him the truth, to get it out and let things fall where they may, but another part was terrified of doing that. She'd put him in such a bad position. He'd have to turn her in. He'd have to call the Feds and tell them where she was. And if he didn't, if he chose not to, he would be putting everything he had on the line. His job, maybe even his own freedom.

She glanced at Adam, thankful he was watching the road, and she admitted to herself right then that she could love him. He was the type of man she'd hoped to meet one day, but now… "I shouldn't even be here. If my car hadn't broken down, I'd be long gone."

"To where?"

"I don't know. Someplace," she said and drew away from his touch. She couldn't stand it when all she wanted to do was hold on to him. "Anywhere."

They were coming to the town, and Adam drew back to clutch the wheel with both hands. "To Illinois?"

She looked away, her heart hammering. "No, I can't. I mean, I don't want to." That was such a lie. When she'd said she couldn't, that had been the truth.

"Why? What's going on there that made you leave in the first place?"

He'd hit the jackpot and she couldn't even form the words to answer him. She knew he'd turned to look at her, but he didn't speak again. He just waited and drove. "Just problems," she finally said and moved closer to the door.

Adam was silent until they got to the inn and he pulled in to park. He left the truck idling and rested his arm along the back of the seat. "Do you want to tell me what's going on?"

More than anything, but she couldn't. It was her life and her mess, and she wouldn't drag him into it. She knew he was an honorable man, that integrity would be everything to him, and if she was so self-indulgent as to spill everything, it would destroy even the memories she was going to leave with.

"No."

"All right…maybe, someday, if you come back to Wolf Lake, I can take you to the old man's land where he found the turquoise or we can go up to the lake. When the snow's gone."

She swallowed hard and didn't say anything. He knew she wouldn't be back. He must know that, but he kept up the charade. When the snow was gone, she'd be nowhere around here, and he'd just be a memory stored in a beautiful stone.

"You…you're going back to Dallas, aren't you?"

Adam seemed taken aback by that, but said, "For now, and you're driving off into the unknown."

She grimaced at his words. They were the stark truth. She was going into the unknown and she'd be doing it alone. Her choice, totally. And just because she cared so much about Adam, she knew that was her only choice.

She felt the seat shift and she thought Adam was getting out, but he wasn't. He came closer to her, his hand lowering to the nape of her neck and his other hand lifted to cup her chin. "You don't have to do this, whatever it is, by yourself," he said on a strangled whisper.

She felt the burn of tears again, but this

time she didn't try to fight them. She knew she couldn't win. They slipped down her cheeks as she looked up at Adam. She didn't just care about this man—she loved him. Heaven help her, but she'd found that love that she knew instinctively was her one and only, and she'd have to walk away.

"Hey," he said, his warm breath brushing across her skin. "Don't cry, please." His lips found hers.

The contact filled her world, pushing out everything, including her sanity. His fingers stroked her hair, her cheek, and for one moment of pure need, she answered his kiss with hers. Everything she felt was in that connection, then she made herself stop.

She pushed back, collected her things and fumbled with the handle until the door swung open. "Faith," Adam said, "I meant it. I want to help."

"Goodbye," she said in a rush as she slipped out and her feet hit the snowy ground. She got to the door of the inn and made the mistake of looking back. Adam was still in the truck, his hands on the steering wheel, just watching her, not moving.

"Goodbye," she whispered into the wind and went inside.

She hurried across to the stairs and didn't pause, hoping to get up to her room without seeing anyone. She made it, got the door open and stepped inside when she heard someone downstairs. She took several breaths to calm her heartbeat, then sat down on the bed, and dropping her purse on the floor at her feet, she opened the carved box and took out the stone.

The perfectly polished turquoise lay on her open palm, and now she understood why it was shaped like a teardrop. Closing her hand around the small stone, she cried.

CHAPTER FIFTEEN

ADAM HAD GONE over and over what he could do and what he would do until dawn came, and he put in a call to his partner in Dallas. He gave him a list of things to track down for him, and after showering and dressing, he went into the main house to check on his dad, then wished he hadn't.

Herbert Carson was in a foul mood, complaining about the fact that he couldn't drive yet and that he needed to rest. Being a recovering alcoholic had given an edge to his dad that flared up from time to time, but he'd never lost his sobriety. Adam finally left, knowing his mother would keep his father in line, and he had things to do.

He'd thought about this all night. While he drove to town, he checked in with his partner, Ray, in Dallas and wasn't surprised to find out that Baron Little was the head of

Faith's father's defense team. But there was little else that Ray had found. That was okay with Adam; he didn't want Ray any more involved, especially if this came to a head.

Still, Ray promised to keep checking on the list. When Adam got to Main Street, he stopped at the inn. He didn't give up on much that was important to him, professionally and personally. That was an asset as a cop and in his personal life. He wasn't about to give up on Jack. He wasn't going to give up on Faith, either. He had until four o'clock, when Dent would release her car, and he intended to make those hours count.

While he waited for answers from Ray, he wasn't going to stop hoping that Faith might confide in him. He got out of the truck and went inside the inn. Mallory was there, writing in the ledger on the desk. "Hey, there," Adam said, going over to her. "Is Faith upstairs?"

"No, she left."

He heart lurched. "She's gone?"

"She went to the general store, then Dent's to push him to get her car finished."

"She's still in town, then?"

"Yes, but not for long. As soon as the car's

fixed, she's going, and Dent said he can get it done today."

"Thanks," Adam said, then hurried toward the door.

"Adam, do you want me to give her a message?"

He stopped and thought. "Do you have some paper and a pen?"

"Sure," she said and took out a sheet of paper with the inn's logo on it, and a pen.

Adam wrote a note to Faith, folded it, put it in a small envelope Mallory offered him, then sealed it. "Make sure she gets this the minute she gets back."

"Sure," she said and laid it on the desk. "Don't worry about it."

"Thanks," he said. He left and climbed into his truck. A glance at his phone on the seat told him he'd missed a call from Ray. He called back, and Ray answered on the first ring.

"Hey, it's me," Adam said.

"I've got something. It doesn't make much sense to me because I don't know what you're up to, but I thought you ought to know anyway."

Adam listened to Ray. "Good, that's good,"

he told him. "Can you keep digging and get me a direct number for that attorney, Little?"

"Sure," Ray muttered. "But I don't walk on water."

"Shoot, and here I've been telling everyone you do," Adam said.

Ray hung up with a promise to get back to Adam when he found what he was looking for.

Adam looked up and down the street and couldn't see Faith anywhere. He backed out and slowly drove toward Manaw's Garage. When he neared it, he spotted Faith walking out from the first service bay, then turned with her head down, walking in the direction of the inn. Her hands were stuffed in her pockets, and her attention seemed to be on her boots.

He pulled in by the gas pumps, got out of the truck and cut across the gravel to head after Faith. Then he remembered the last time he'd chased her and thought better of it. She seemed intent on getting somewhere, so he backed off and just watched her walk. He'd let her go, for now.

"Adam?"

He turned and saw Dent wiping greasy

hands on an equally greasy rag, coming toward him. "The car's done," he said in a low voice when he got close. "I just need to snap the plug wires into the harness to finish it."

"Good. Just let it be for now, and I'll get back to you soon. This might be done sooner than four o'clock."

Dent nodded, but said, "You know, brother, that little lady is making me feel like the Grinch."

"This means everything to me and I hope it will to her."

"She's desperate to leave this place," Dent called after him.

"I know," he called back.

He got in his truck, determined he knew what to do. He drove in the direction of the police station, relieved to see John's car parked outside. He went straight to John's office and closed the door. "I need a favor, John, a huge favor, friend to friend, nothing less."

John looked up, took one look at Adam's face. "What did you do?"

"That's what I need to talk to you about, but there can't be anyone else in on this."

John stared hard at him, then sat back

in his chair. "Sit down, friend, and tell me what's going on."

Adam did more. "Totally off the record?"

John didn't hesitate. "Friend to friend," he said.

FAITH WANTED TO SIT in Dent's garage and just wait for the car to be done. But she knew she couldn't, though she didn't want to run into anyone, either, least of all Adam. Walking alone, she kept her head low and held tightly to the carved box in her pocket. It had come to feel like a talisman for her. She concentrated on getting back to the inn without seeing anyone, but knew it was risky.

So she moved off to a side street, circled back and wound up at the inn just like before when she'd gone the wrong way. She studied the inn, then during a break in traffic, she darted across the street and got inside. No one seemed to notice her. Except for Mallory.

"Glad you got back," she said, coming downstairs, where Faith had started up them.

Mallory waited for her to join her, then held out an envelope to her. "I was about to put this under your door before I went out. It's from Adam."

The envelope was light in Faith's hand, and she wasn't sure what to do.

"Adam said to make sure you got it." Mallory paused at the top of the stairs. "When will you be leaving?"

"By four, I think"

"Good, I'll try to be back by then." Mallory hesitated. "I'm really going to miss you."

The catch in her voice almost did Faith in. The hug that came next made it hard for Faith. "I'll miss all of you."

Mallory patted her back and said, "Please, come on back this way again?"

She would have loved nothing more than to come back, but she couldn't lie. "I don't think I can, but I'll never forget you."

Mallory stood back and swiped at her eyes. "Darn, I hate getting all misty." She gave a weak smile. "You drive carefully."

Faith nodded and, clutching the envelope, went into her room. She ignored the note while she finished packing, but when she was ready, the only thing left in the room that was hers was the note. She slowly opened it and unfolded the single sheet of paper inside.

Faith,
Don't leave before I get there.
We have to talk.

A scrawl at the bottom must have said *Adam*. She wasn't sure, partly because it was more style than form and partly because her eyes were blurring. She carefully folded the paper, pushed it back into the envelope. Her first instinct was to leave it there, but it was the only tangible thing of Adam's that she had. She pushed it into the pocket of her jacket, which she was still wearing, along with the carved box.

"Done," she said, and then she called Dent. She knew the man was tired of her pressuring him, but she didn't hesitate to phone him again.

When he answered, she said, "Hi, this is Faith Arden."

"Yes, I thought it might be." She didn't know if he was being teasing or sarcastic. She didn't care.

"How much longer?" she asked.

"Tell you what, if you don't call me again, I might be able to get it done sooner. That way you get what you want faster, and I'll be in a better mood when you pay the bill." He laughed at his own statement. "Does that sound like a deal?" he asked.

She smiled a bit herself. "Yes, that's a deal," she said.

"Wonderful. I'll see you soon."

She hung up.

So this meant that she'd be gone soon. She should have felt relieved, but oddly, she couldn't begin to figure out what she was feeling. She glanced at the clock: 2:00 p.m. She had a couple more hours to get through.

ADAM CHECKED THE CLOCK and had only forty-five minutes to get to Dent's to find Faith. He walked out of John's office, got to his truck and his phone rang. He flipped it open and answered it. "Ray, have you got it?"

"I do," his partner said. He read off a phone number, then added, "He's waiting for your call but can't hang around too long."

"I owe you," Adam said. Once he was in the truck, he punched in the number for Baron Little's private line. When a man answered, identifying himself as the attorney, Adam introduced himself, then told him what he wanted to do. The man listened patiently and then said, "I can't tell you anything about the case or about my client."

"Well, you can listen, can't you?"

"Yes, but—"

"Just listen."

"You've got five minutes, and the clock is ticking."

FAITH'S NERVES WERE RAW. She couldn't wait any longer. Having packed all of her belongings, she went downstairs intending to ask Mallory if she could leave them there while she took one last trip to Dent's. But Mallory wasn't there. So she pushed her bags behind the desk and left.

She got to the garage and thought for a minute it was locked up tight. But the one bay door was up and her car was there unlocked. She was ready to call for Dent when a woman came up to her.

She looked about forty, was full-figured with dark skin and short black hair. She smiled at Faith. "Faith Arden?"

"Yes."

"I'm Dent's wife. He had to go to fix a flat at the last minute, and he left me here to meet you at four." She glanced at her wristwatch.

"A few minutes early, but that's all good. I have some last minute shopping to do for the kids." She pulled a piece of paper out of her pocket and handed it to Faith. "Dent said you'd settle this."

Faith took the bill, handed Mrs. Dent the money and was rewarded by being handed the keys to her car. Within five minutes she was back at the inn, parking her perfectly running car out front and going in to get her luggage. Mallory wasn't back yet, and no one was behind the desk, not even Willie G.

She left an envelope on the desk with her payment for what she owed for her room and included a bit extra for Mallory. She propped it against the old ledger, then took her things out to the car. It was still several minutes before four, and she waited. But Adam didn't show up. She fingered the steering wheel, looked around, then knew she was being stupid. She had to leave.

There wasn't any black truck racing down the street or a tall man with a Stetson striding toward her. She hadn't wanted to see him again anyway, she reasoned as she put the car in Reverse and backed out. That was a total lie, but it was the way it should be. Over and done. Then she turned to head out of town, going northwest.

She was finally driving away from Wolf Lake, and she should be thrilled, but all Faith felt was that she was driving away from everything good in her life and everything she desperately wanted. As she passed the hospital, she pulled over and let the car idle. She took the small case out of her pocket, lifted the turquoise teardrop out of its nest and closed her fingers around it, holding it tightly in one hand. She tossed the case onto the passenger seat and drove off.

She'd go west, then north, up into Colorado. Once she found a place to stay for the night, she'd figure out where to go from there. Honestly, she didn't care where she ended up as long as she kept to her own rules. She would never again let herself get involved with a town full of characters and a tall, dark-haired man who only showed her what she'd never have. The love of her life had come and gone, and she wasn't so sure that she would survive in one piece. She knew her heart wouldn't.

She kept going and found the highway heading north. The town was gone. Snow began to fall, driven by a blustery wind. Gray clouds blotted out the sunlight. She felt the turquoise in her hand and rubbed its smooth surface with her fingertips. Memories. "That's all I have now," she said as she went into a sharp curve and felt the car's tires leave the pavement.

ADAM PULLED AWAY from the police station after his conversation with the attorney with only ten minutes to get to Dent's. While he drove, he called the garage, but the phone went to an answering machine. He hung up and tried the inn. No one answered there, either. When he got to the inn and didn't see any cars out front, he parked, jogged to the door and went inside.

No one was at the desk, but he saw a single envelope propped against the register. *Mallory* was written on the front of it. He stood there, called out to Mallory, but there was no answer, so he took the stairs two at a time, got to Faith's room and found it stripped of everything that would have shown Faith had been there.

Quickly, he went back down and met Mallory coming in. "Hey, Adam," she said, looking past him. "I gave Faith your note. Is she still here?"

"No."

"Darn, I wanted to get back before she left."

"Me, too," he muttered as she spotted the envelope. She picked it up, opened it and took out a number of bills, then a piece of notepaper. She unfolded it, read it and handed it to Adam.

> Mallory,
> You never gave me the final bill, and I had to leave, so I made a guess at what it was and added 10 percent. I hope that covers what I owe you. I don't know how to thank you for all your kindnesses. Please tell everyone goodbye for me.
> Merry Christmas.
> Faith.

He dropped it onto the desk. "Have you seen Dent?"

She looked at him, thankfully not asking him any questions he didn't want to answer. "Saw him about half an hour ago on his way to a customer who had a flat tire. His wife was holding down the fort at the garage."

He called and spoke with Dent's wife, confirming what Mallory had told him. She didn't know which way Faith was headed. The only other person he could think of was Oscar. If anyone had seen Faith leave, it would be him. Adam ignored the truck and jogged over to the general store. Oscar was locking up, but true to form, he knew everything about everyone. He'd seen Faith leave about twenty minutes earlier, and she'd been going west out of town. Adam checked the clock. Depending how she was driving, she had a decent head start on him.

He ran back to his truck, climbed in, revved it up and turned out onto the street to head west. Since there were only two ways out of town to the west and one headed to the res, she had to be on the state route that cut west, then north and up into Colorado eventually. He drove as quickly as he could, hoping the snow would stop, but the farther he went, the less that seemed likely to happen. Thick, wet flakes made it hard to see the road. Only faint impressions of anyone else were visible. He slowed more and more as the weather deteriorated.

Hindsight being twenty-twenty, he wished he'd just told Faith what he knew about her and let things fall where they may. But he couldn't have. Not until he'd cleared up a lot with the attorney, and now he was free to tell her everything. Ironically, she was gone, and for all he knew, she wouldn't ever return. His windshield wipers were laboring to keep the glass clear, and on the curves he slowed to a crawl.

Why hadn't he just told her that he cared about her? Why hadn't he begged her to stay? Better yet, he thought, why hadn't he simply told her the truth? He'd been so focused on her being truthful with him, but he'd done his share of lying to her, small things, but important things.

He pulled over when he lost sight of the road on a curve. The snow let up gradually and he pushed through and came out onto a relatively straight stretch of road that climbed higher. He barely stopped himself from standing on the brake.

A car that looked like the one Faith had been driving was twenty feet ahead, nose down in a ditch. He could see the impression under the new snow where the tires had fought for traction, then sailed out of control. A fear he'd never known he was capable of feeling tore at him as he jumped out of the idling truck and made his way through the drifting snow to get to the disabled car.

He half slid into the ditch, hit the driver's door with the soles of his boots, barely avoiding putting his foot through the window, and he came to a jarring stop. The windows were iced and foggy, and Adam reached to grab the door handle to leverage himself up to his feet, where he immediately started to sink up to his knees in the snow. He got his balance finally, pulled the handle with a vicious jerk and heard it click and give. He grabbed the frame and forced the door back halfway. He had enough room to look inside.

It was empty and he stood back, looking frantically around, not seeing anything but snow and ice-laden pines. Bracing himself on the driver's seat, he could see something on the floor of the passenger side. He pushed farther in, awkwardly reaching down to touch the smooth finish of the tiny turquoise teardrop.

Closing his hand over it, he hoisted himself out of the car. He couldn't remember the last time he'd felt panic drive him, but it did now. He looked down at the stone in his hand as snow fell on it and he slowly curled his fingers around it. He turned and screamed for Faith at the top of his lungs.

He waited, willing a response that never came. He twisted around, getting his balance, then climbed hand over hand up the sharp incline of the ditch. He made it to the road and almost slipped more than once as he hurried to his truck. He finally made it, reached into the truck to get his cell phone and punched in 911.

"Nine one one. What is the emergency you're reporting?" a female voice asked.

He quickly told her about the car going off the road, and she cut him off. "Yes, that has been reported, sir."

He forced himself to keep calm and remain in control. "What was reported?"

"Sir, I can't give that information out to you."

Adam didn't hesitate. "I'm a cop with the Dallas P.D. I used to be a cop in Wolf Lake.

There's been an accident and I need some information. Now, what was reported?"

"A single car went off the road at marker 27. It was found by a patrol car out of the Pine Cross substation about half an hour ago. Went out of control on a curve and was disabled."

"What about the driver?" he asked, literally holding his breath until the operator spoke again.

"A female was found and taken to Pine Cross."

He braced himself. "Any injuries reported?"

"No, none on the report. They took the lady to the substation in the town, then got her to the This Is It Motel. They got a tow truck ordered to retrieve the vehicle, but with this weather, it's going to be a while."

"Do you have a name for the driver?"

"Yes, sir, Faith Arden."

He exhaled a breath and closed his eyes for a second before asking for directions to the substation in Pine Cross. When he hung up, he let himself breathe, and then he climbed into the truck, swiped at the snow clinging to the leather at his shoulders. He put the truck in gear and drove toward Pine Cross. Faith was all right. She wasn't hurt.

His relief was monumental, and in that moment, he understood just a fraction of the fear and loss Jack must have felt the night Robyn had been taken from him. Adam never wanted to feel that way again. Never.

FAITH SAT ALONE in a beige-on-beige room, stuck in Pine Cross, waiting for another mechanic to tell her when or if her car could be driven again. Cursing the stupid car did no good, and tears weren't there for her. Her eyes were dry, and she felt almost numb. She'd known Christmas would be lost to her this year, and she'd been right. Christmas Eve was even worse. In this room, with a prepackaged cheese sandwich and warm cola to celebrate, she stared at the TV that didn't seem to have sound. Just as well, because she'd watched this particular movie at least a dozen times. *It's a Wonderful Life.* She almost laughed, but no sound came from her, either.

She clicked off the TV, pushed the sandwich away and vowed to get through this.

She'd find a way, another town, another place, and make very sure she kept to herself.

When a knock at the door overrode the whistling wind outside, she assumed it was the clerk bringing her a list of car-rental places that served this area. He'd promised to find it for her when she'd checked in. She got up to pad in her stockinged feet to the door and called out, "Who's there?"

"Me," a voice she knew all too well responded.

"No, no," she whispered. *He can't be here.*

A heavy knock sounded on the flimsy door. "Faith, please, open up."

She offered up a silent prayer to help her handle this well. When she opened the door, Adam stood there, the snow falling heavily behind him. His hair was touched by the whiteness, the Stetson nowhere in sight, and more snow covered his shoulders. His dark eyes stared at her, and he didn't say a word for what seemed like forever. Then without warning, he stepped toward her and pulled her into his arms in a fierce hug.

Even though he brought wetness and cold with him, Faith thought that hug from Adam was the most precious thing anyone had given her. She closed her eyes, pressed her cheek to his chest and let him hold her. He must have hooked the door with his boot, because it flew shut, and they were in the silence of the room.

He'd followed her, and she hated him for it. No, she loved him for it, but she hated him doing it. She couldn't let him be here. She couldn't. She pushed back and away from his embrace. "Leave," she said, her voice unsteady and less than convincing.

"I'm not going anywhere."

"Please, please, just go," she said, desperate to have him gone.

He quietly came to her, hunkering down, but he didn't touch her. "Faith, listen to me and believe what I'm saying to you." There was gentleness in his voice that was almost her undoing.

She couldn't deal with that. What she wanted was to be alone, but more than that, for Adam to be safe and not involved in the damage from her life. That was all she'd ever wanted since she'd known what she felt for him. But he shattered that hope.

"I can't go anywhere until we talk honestly. You owe me that."

She closed her eyes and clasped her hands tightly together. “Adam, please don’t do this.”

She sensed movement and opened her eyes to see him moving away from her. Yes, she was glad that he was going, but at the same time it also hurt her. Then he shattered her thinking by grabbing the desk chair and spinning it around so the back was facing Faith. He straddled the seat and rested his chin on his crossed arms. His dark eyes never left her face.

“There’s nothing to say.” The words almost choked her.

“Okay, you don’t have to talk, but I do.”

He started speaking in a low voice, his eyes narrowing as if he was having trouble saying what he seemed bent on telling her. “I came after you when I found you’d left Mallory’s. Oscar saw you leave, told me the direction and I headed out. When I found your car…” He sat straighter and stared at his hands. “I…I thought you were dead or dying.”

She saw his expression change to heartache. “I have never been so scared in my life.” His voice became hoarse. “Never. Not even on the job. Never.” His eyes found hers again, and she almost flinched at the intensity in the darkness. "I could face down anything, but I couldn't face the possibility that you were gone. Really gone."

"I…I had to leave," she muttered. "I had to."

His eyes narrowed even more, and she felt as if he could barely endure looking at her. "No, you chose to." He exhaled in a rush. "You ran because you didn't trust me enough to tell me why Faith Sizemore was hiding in Wolf Lake…."

CHAPTER SIXTEEN

FAITH STARED AT ADAM, stunned. "You know… you know."

He didn't respond, just kept watching her and she felt as if she were suffocating. She moved, bumping her knee against his knee as she stood. The pain shot up her leg, and she jerked sideways, away from Adam.

What was she going to do? Run out into the night with no jacket, no luggage, no wallet?

Her nightmare had come true. Adam knew who she was; there would be no more running. Everything was over.

She had to force herself to look at him, and when she did she admitted that he had to hear the truth.

She moved awkwardly, her knee still stinging. At the window, she pushed the worn drapes aside. The storm was still raging. She kept her back to the room and Adam. She couldn't do this while looking at him, seeing the repulsion that would surely surface on his face.

He had been worried she'd died, but he had no idea how close she was to dying inside at that moment.

She sneaked one glance at Adam, but it did her in. She slid slowly down, her back brushing the wall, until she ended up sitting on the floor. She hugged her arms around her legs when she drew them to her chest and stared at the faded carpet. "What do you know exactly?"

He didn't speak, and she had to look up again. He was by the bed, slipping off his damp jacket, tossing it on the abandoned chair. "Why don't you just tell me the truth? That's all I've ever wanted from you instead of the lies."

She pressed her forehead to her knees and fought for control. She didn't want to cry in front of him again. Not now.

What Adam wanted was the one thing she feared the most. But she finally managed to force out words whose power to hurt and destroy increased as she spoke them aloud.

"I left Chicago twenty-four days ago. My father, he's all I've ever had, and I would do anything for him." Closing her eyes, she kept talking. "And I have, I am. I left Chicago because the grand jury was being seated to get indictments against my father." She grimaced and continued, the charges against her father burned into her memory. "They were expected to ask for indictments for securities fraud, investment-adviser fraud, wire fraud and international money laundering.

"The grand jury is hearing testimony right now, as far as I know. An indictment is almost inevitable. The prosecutor was going to subpoena me to testify because I worked at the firm. Daughter of a partner." She shrugged weakly. "I couldn't do that to Dad. So I took off, changed my name and left—"

"So you ran and figured if you kept moving, the Feds couldn't find you, at least not soon enough for grand-jury testimony and probably not for actual trial testimony."

Adam had sat down beside her. "I thought I could make it work," she admitted, "and I'd never have to testify."

He narrowed his eyes on her. "What do you know that's so damning for your dad, or did you leave just in case something you didn't know about came up and they nailed you?"

She shook her head. "I just didn't want to hurt Dad."

"Of course not, but you could have stayed and testified and left the prosecutor holding the bag when it turned out you didn't know anything."

"I couldn't do it." She wouldn't tell anyone about what she knew. Not even this man, whom she could finally acknowledge she loved with all her heart. "I just didn't ever expect to find a place like Wolf Lake and people who didn't know how to stay away or how to not help someone in need."

He smiled. "Even Willie G. was worried about you getting your rest and told me to take good care of you." He saw her surprise, but didn't say anything about it. "So you landed right in the middle of a gang of people who didn't understand the concept of keeping out of their neighbor's business." He tapped her knee with his forefinger. "I have to tell you, you can't do anything about them wanting to help or being involved in your life. Wolf Lake isn't a place where you can blend in and stay low."

She swiped at his finger to break the contact, then stumbled to her feet. She sat on the edge of the mattress. "You don't know the half of it. When I lost my wallet, I thought if you found it and looked inside, being a cop, you'd turn me in as soon as possible." She paused and looked at him. "Is that how you found out who I am? You went through my wallet and pretended to find it by accident?"

"No, I'm not that good an actor," he said. "I'm just a cop who does the grunt work. Actually, it was knowing your birth date and that you were probably from Illinois that helped me. Enough to get me going anyway."

She shook her head. She'd never even thought about her birthday. One of the best days she'd had and it had led to this. "Yes, you're a cop," she murmured.

"Yep, sworn to uphold the law," he muttered, coming across to the bed.

"Exactly. You've got a job to do, and you'll do it. I know that."

"So what scenario is the right one about what's going on with you?" he asked her, and she drew a blank.

"Just what you said, me running away, getting out of Chicago and staying away as long as I could before they'd find me."

"I know that. It's what I would have done if I couldn't be there. But I'm talking about the reason behind you not being able to stay. What are you hiding? What do you know that you don't want to give to the prosecution?"

She'd said enough, and anything she said, he'd repeat to the prosecutors sooner or later. He'd have to. "Nothing."

He paced back and forth for a moment, then came back to where she sat. He was close enough for her to feel his strength, his warmth. "Faith, yes, you can. I'll tell you why. I talked to Baron Little."

"What?" she gasped. "How? But he couldn't talk to you."

"Oh, he didn't tell me much of anything, but he listened while I explained my situation, and he gave me some suggestions about what to do."

"How did you find him?"

"His name was in some of the online coverage of the arrests. I got his direct number and he agreed to hear me out. That's why

I didn't get to the inn before you left." He gave her a glance, then said in a low voice, "I thought you'd wait."

"What do you want?" she asked.

"All I've wanted from the first is for you to trust me enough to tell me the truth. Then I realized what you were thinking. I'm a cop, sworn to do my duty, and that would mean turning you in if I knew where you were and why you were there."

She started to shake and couldn't stop. "I wanted to tell you, I really did, but I couldn't." She felt as if she were drowning and couldn't even reach for safety. "I'm not good at this fugitive thing, or lying."

"No, you're not. You're too easy to read, and you have the worst possible thing for a fugitive to have—a conscience."

"Thanks," she muttered.

"Hey, in my mind, those traits are good, but for survival, you need more deviousness."

She thought he was making fun of her, but there was no smile on his face. "Why are you here?" she asked bluntly.

"To get you."

"Are the Feds on their way for me? Did you tell them everything?"

"No one's on the way. It's Christmas Eve and only an idiot would be out in this weather." He pointed to her, then back at himself. "Make that two idiots."

She'd been an idiot to think she could have escaped merely by leaving Wolf Lake. "You really need to go, get back to your place and forget all about this, everything."

"And what about you?" he asked.

The room suddenly felt colder to her. "One way or the other, I'll just go until I can stop."

"You know," he said, not showing any signs of leaving, "when I found that car, I understood a bit about what Jack went through when Robyn had her accident. I mean, you're here with me now, but that fear was debilitating, thinking something awful had happened to you."

She looked at him, and he was hunched forward, his head down. She touched his shoulder. "I'm sorry. I didn't know what to do. I had to leave." Tears were there, so close to falling. "I knew if you found out, you could lose your job if you didn't let the authorities know, or you could lose your freedom. I couldn't let that happen to you, not to you, never." She moved closer to him, her hand slipping down his arm until she was touching his hand. She didn't care that the tears were very real now, sliding down her cheeks. "Do you understand?" she choked out. "Please tell me you do."

"Yes, I do." His hand turned in hers and his fingers twined with hers, anchoring her for that moment in time. "I really do." He glanced at her, his eyes touched by pain, and it made her heart ache.

"I know you need to take care of this, call someone, report me, whatever, but would you at least give me a head start?"

"Oh, Faith," he said, pulling her to him, gathering her to his chest.

"Just give me a chance," she sobbed, balling his shirt in her hands.

"Please, please, tell me the truth," he said barely above a whisper.

ADAM FELT FAITH break their embrace and he let her go, but she didn't get up and move away from him. She stared into his face, tears still clinging to her lashes, and she touched a finger to his jawline, tracing it. "Making memories," she said, then seemed to stiffen as she wiped her eyes. "Okay, it doesn't matter anymore." He'd wanted her to trust him, but now she just looked defeated. He hated it.

Staring down at the floor, she told him slowly about hearing her father and his partners six months before the raid, talking about taking care of the account and the client. How her dad was going to fix things.

She looked exhausted when she finished and Adam felt it, too. He touched her cheek, smoothing back the curls that clung to her damp skin as he asked, "Did you ask him about what you heard?"

"No, I couldn't."

He understood why. "Afraid he'd lie to you, or afraid you'd heard it right?"

She closed her eyes, and he felt her tremble where his fingertips lingered on her cheek. "He'd never lie to me," she said.

"So you think you heard it right, that your assumption was correct?"

"Yes, I do," she replied and reached for his hand, holding it tightly to her as she kept speaking. She told him about her file searches and what she'd found. "It's the truth. And it's horrible."

"So your dad is either a dupe and his partners used him to cover up for them, or he did what you think he did, and you won't toss him under the bus?"

"You really are a cop, aren't you?" she muttered.

"No, I'm not."

Those blue eyes turned to him, but her hold never faltered. "What?"

"I'm not a cop. I resigned, effective the day John stopped you for speeding. I didn't know anything about you then, not even your real name, which," he said, "makes me just a citizen with no obligation to do anything about the mess Faith Marie Sizemore got herself into."

A frown tugged fine lines between her eyes, and when she started to pull her hand free, he held on to her for dear life. "Is this some slick interrogation method to get me to spill even more of my guts than I already have?"

"I quit the force. I told you I was going to make changes, and this is one of them."

"So you're not a cop anymore?"

"Not for the moment. I've been thinking of talking to John about sticking around Wolf Lake for a while, though."

"You mean that?"

"I'm not lying. And I don't and won't lie to you about anything...ever."

She exhaled, her hand staying in his. "And are you going to tell everyone in Wolf Lake who I am and what I've done?"

"No, that's up to you, if or when you decide you want to."

He stood and pulled her to her feet. With inches separating them, he shifted to lay both hands on her shoulders. "Thank you for telling me the truth," he said. "That means a lot to me. But I have one more question."

She took a shaky breath. "What's that?"

This was it. Everything was on the table now. "Why didn't you ask me why I said I finally understood something about how Jack felt when he lost Robyn?"

"I don't know. I guess I thought you were mad at me for taking off, and when you thought there had been trouble, you..."

"Ask me now," he said evenly.

She shook her head. "It's not important."

It was life-and-death for him. "Oh, yes, it is. Ask me."

"Okay, what was that all about?"

He didn't realize that there were other fears

in him. Now he was fearful that he'd been wrong about everything, that he'd jumped to his own conclusions. But he couldn't stop now. "Because I thought I'd lost you forever, and I knew, right then, if I had lost you, I wasn't sure that I could keep going."

Her blue eyes filled with tears again as she asked, "Why?"

"Because I love you," he said, startled at how easy it was to say words he'd avoided all his life.

Faith raised a hand, its touch soft on his cheek and as unsteady as he felt inside. "If things were different, if I wasn't who I am, if..." Her words faded and she drew back her hand.

"No, I love you, and it's that simple. It can be that simple, and it is that simple."

"But what about all that mess in Chicago?"

"What about it?" he asked.

"You can't get pulled into that, no matter what."

"No, I can't, but I can walk into it and help you. I told you I've talked to Baron, and—"

"But he doesn't know what I heard."

"Seems he's the best there is. You should

go back. Be totally honest with him, tell him everything."

"No, I can't."

He reached up to cup her chin gently. "Trust me. It's the smartest move on your part to do that as soon as possible."

When she hesitated, he worried he'd gotten everything wrong, but when she spoke, the worry faded. "Yes, I can do that, and I do trust you. It's just scary to think of doing the very thing I've been running away from."

"I know it's scary, but I'll be with you every step of the way," he said. "I will never let you down, never."

He saw that moment in her eyes when she made her decision, and thankfully, it was the one he'd hoped for. Looking right at him, Faith said, "I love you, too. And I promise I'll never lie to you again."

He hugged her, sweeping her off her feet and into his arms. She kissed him passionately, lovingly.

She drew back, whispered, "My one and only love." Her smile was brilliant and he matched it with his own.

"And now for one last thing," he said. "Faith, reach into my shirt pocket if you can."

Faith put her fingers in the pocket and found the memory stone. Her eyes were wide with surprise.

"I had this in my hand when the car went into the ditch, and it was gone after everything stopped. I thought it was lost forever." She kissed him quickly. "Thank you, thank you, thank you," she whispered between each kiss.

"I told you, I need to keep finding stuff for you," he said, teasing. "I love your way of saying thank-you."

They were silent for a long while, the kiss they shared an affirmation of all the trust and love two people could have.

"I love you, Adam, but I have to get back to Chicago, talk to Baron and turn myself in. I've got to get through all of this and settle it once and for all. Then we can figure out where we're going."

"Lady, at first I was willing to let you go do what you had to do in Chicago and trust you'd come back to me when the snow was gone." He kissed her quickly, then said, "But I found out I'm not that noble. And whether the snow is falling or not, I want you with me."

"But it's not just me. It's my dad, and I've broken the law. I'll probably be in real trouble when I go back. I don't know what's going to happen to any of us."

Adam could feel her hurt and frustration with respect to her father, her fear for the future for both of them, but mostly, he couldn't stand to think that she thought she had to go through all of that alone. Still…it wasn't all about him, not anymore. "Listen, if you need to do this on your own, I'll wait in Wolf Lake for you," he offered, the hardest thing he'd ever said to anyone in his life.

"Really?"

"Really. But you have to know one thing."

She stood very still in front of him. "What?" she asked.

"Nothing counts in this world without you. I came back home, and for the first time in my life, I feel as if I want to stay in Wolf Lake. But not without you."

She didn't move, but her eyes closed and fresh tears trailed down her face. "Oh, shoot," she breathed.

"What?"

"I can't just go and leave you back here," she said, as if that made her annoyed. "And if you go, I don't know how you'll cope, how I'll cope."

"Together," he said. "I've never been to Chicago and I want to be there with you. I love you, Faith Sizemore, and I've never said that to any other woman in my life." He reached for her, pulled her to him, and she held on to him fiercely.

"Did you hear me? Do you understand that this is once in a lifetime for me?"

"Yes. Yes." A smile started on her lips and spread to her still-damp eyes. "Now, hear me—I love you, Adam Carson, and I very selfishly want you to be with me no matter what's happening."

"Yes," he said, ready to do the honorable thing, but so thankful she didn't take him up on his offer to do it all alone.

Faith stayed in his arms as the wind and snow howled outside, while inside, promises were given and plans were made. Adam kissed her, then drew back and smiled down at her. She touched the dimple with the tip of her finger as she said, "Merry Christmas, Adam," and he knew that he was home and that this was going to be the best Christmas ever.

EPILOGUE

Chicago, Illinois

THE DAY BEFORE New Year's Eve, the city was hit with the biggest snowstorm of the season. Chicago streets were framed with drifts of snow almost as high as car roofs. The streets were eventually cleared and the sun was shining from a late-afternoon sky.

Two people stepped out of a cab in front of a beautifully restored town house a block from the lake. They held hands as they made their way off of the slippery street, through a gap in the snow piles and onto the walkway that was still covered by a dusting of snow. Adam, in jeans, boots and a thigh-length leather trench coat, held on to Faith. He could feel the hesitancy in her now that they were almost back to where her journey had begun.

Thankfully, the combination of the unprecedented snowfall and the coming New Year had combined to rid the front entrance of all but two media people. Those two were sitting in an idling van parked about twenty feet from the house. But when they saw a tall stranger heading for the place with a short, curly-haired woman also dressed in jeans, boots and a rough denim jacket, they shouted at them to get their attention. After they took a photo, they settled back into the relative comfort of their van.

As Faith and Adam got to the front gate, a security man who seemed to come out of nowhere met them, unlocked the heavy door and pulled it forward. He didn't speak, just nodded to Faith as she passed by still holding on to Adam. The door to the house wasn't locked and so in they went. Faith tried to take it all in, and Adam followed her.

No one was there to greet them, so after they got out of their heavy jackets, Faith took Adam's hand and led him upstairs. The library door was partially ajar and she pushed it farther back until it thudded softly against the wall. This time she didn't surprise her father. He'd been waiting for hours while their flight had been rerouted because of the storm.

They'd talked and talked on the phone during the journey, and she'd gone over everything with Baron, who was sitting by the desk.

Her dad stood when she walked in, and Faith ached at the tension she could see in him. Without a word, she let go of Adam to step into her father's outstretched arms. "Angel," he murmured. She could feel the relief and regret in his embrace as he held her to him. "I am so sorry. I never knew that you heard us that night." He drew back, his face tight with pain. "It's such a mess. I can't begin to explain what I did, except that I didn't have an option."

Faith tried to smile. "It's all true," she said. She turned to Adam and could see that he ached for her. "We shouldn't have come back," she told him nervously.

Baron lifted his bulk out of the chair he'd been sitting in, stood and faced her and Adam. "Oh, yes, you should have," he said with conviction. "You're the one person who might help mitigate your father's complicity in this wreckage." He frowned at her. "I wish I'd known much earlier about you hearing that confrontation. It could have changed everything."

"Why? If I testify about the meeting, I'll seal my dad's fate. It will prove he knew all about Kenner and actively participated in it. I never should have come back at all."

ADAM KEPT HIMSELF from reaching for Faith, to hold her and give her support. But as he watched, he knew how strong she really was, no matter what happened. "What do you mean?" he asked Baron.

The big man addressed him. "Simply put, Faith is a witness to the coercion her father's partner used to get him to fix the Kenner bungle, to—" he formed air quotes with his fingers "—take care of it. And that if what had been supposedly done came out, they would all turn on him. Also, there was the not-so-implied threat when he spoke to Raymond about Ray's own complicity in the matter and his not surviving close scrutiny without paying for everything. That goes a long way to prove that coercion was used." Baron looked at Faith. "And, you, my dear, you will testify to that on the stand at the trial. You'll be deposed first, put it on the record for discovery, and the prosecutor will arrange the rest."

Faith cast Adam a quizzical glance, and he asked Baron directly, "What does that mean for Raymond?"

"Anything from a conviction and jail time to a plea bargain to minimize the sentence, or some charges being thrown out, all the way down to probation and public service. Our preferred option, of course, would be a dismissal, but that's not going to happen."

Faith held her hand out to Adam. He went to her side, clasping her hand with his. She said, "I ran because I thought what I knew would hurt Dad, and all the time..."

Her voice broke and Adam took her into his arms. "You did what you thought was right, and even so, you're the hero in this piece."

Baron nodded. "Absolutely," he said.

Faith's dad approached her with a satisfied expression on his face. "I am glad this is over for you. I am ashamed of what I've done in the past, and I will do what I have to do now to make it right." To Adam, he said, "I'm sorry you were caught up in this. Though I'm very thankful my daughter has you in her life."

"She always will," Adam murmured and felt Faith squeeze his hand tightly.

Raymond nodded. "Faith tells me that she loves you and that you're trustworthy, honorable, brilliant and you can make a lake appear from a sea of grass."

Adam winked at Faith; he loved the way she could blush. "I get confused with a Good Samaritan all the time, sir, and she still hasn't seen the lake, but soon, very soon, when the snow's gone, she will."

AS THE MEN SPOKE, Faith relaxed. With her dad and Adam, she was standing between the two most important people in her world and knew her father had been right about finding that one true love that only a few people in the world were lucky enough to find. She'd found hers.

"Sit down and get comfortable," her dad suggested, gesturing for all of them to take a seat. "We have a lot to discuss. I'm going to forgo any more apologies and get right to the core of the issue at hand. I will accept whatever punishment I'm given for my complicity in the matter."

"What about Faith?" Adam asked Baron. "What's she facing?"

"Since she came back and will offer to testify about the meeting she overheard, I don't believe they will press any charges against her for taking off as she did."

Faith felt a load lift from her shoulders. She glanced around, grateful that she was back here in her favorite room in the house. So often she'd thought that would never be possible. She touched the pendant she wore nestled to her heart, the tiny turquoise teardrop Adam had set in antique silver for her belated Christmas present. Her bracelet with the charm on it tinkled softly with the movement of her hand. As she looked at Adam, she smiled again. The memories were growing every day they were together, such wonderful memories.

Adam must have felt her looking at him, because he turned right then, saw her hand on the pendant, and he smiled. The single dimple showed up, and Faith knew that he'd been right. Together they could get through anything.

* * * * *

Special Offers

Every month we put together collections and longer reads written by your favourite authors.

Here are some of next month's highlights—and don't miss our fabulous discount online!

On sale 21st February

On sale 28th February

On sale 21st February

Save 20%

on all Special Releases

Find out more at
www.millsandboon.co.uk/specialreleases

Visit us Online

0314/ST/MB461